One Run Too many

One Run Too Many

by

OZ RANDOM

Designed Conviction Publications

www.designedconviction.com

Designed Conviction Publications
Publishers since 2018
A subcompany of Designed Conviction
A Social Enterprise
www.designedconviction.com

ISBN: 978-1-957153-03-2

I would like to dedicate this book to my son. You drive me to be better every day.

I love you

This is OZ, also known as the musician O Zeta. Thanks for picking up my first novel and if you haven't check out my first single On Lock feel free to do so. This is my first venture into singing and writing from behind these bars and I kinda feel like Kanye singing through the wire except I'm singing through the line you know?

I'm originally from Detroit and have always had a talent for singing and writing; neither of which was fully realized until the court sat me down with life without parole.

I'm an optimist though so I find magic in the ordinary and refuse to do anything less than set a pace to be great even from behind these bars.

Look out for my first EP Pain on These Bars and my next two novels Dragon Soul Acceptance and Hidden both of which are coming soon.

Official
Z

Table of Contents

CH1 1

CH2 14

CH3 34

CH4 44

CH5 55

CH6 74

CH7 92

CH8 116

CH9 127

CH10 149

CH11 168

CH12 180

CH13 193

CH14 207

CH15 216

Epilogue 226

CH1

Speed is an aphrodisiac.

I weaved through lackluster evening traffic. The hour meant not many people took up road estate so I zipped along like the roadrunner through a Wile E. Coyote trap.

Nothing compares to watching the speedometer rise past the limits set by some congressman afraid of going too fast or watching as everything becomes a blur as you zoom by. Truthfully, driving often doesn't even become fun for me until after 60 mph's. Granted, that first few seconds when you can accelerate from zero to sixty in less than so many seconds and let the g-forces press your body back into the seat like God's hand against your chest is the beginning of the rush but being able to push beyond that and control a beast on four wheels is the bigger thrill.

Ahead of me a light turned yellow with a line of traffic that most people would've joined. Being able to see patterns in traffic has always allowed me more freedom on the road so I pushed down on the accelerator of my tuned up Neon SRT trusting my skill, loving the sound as the twin turbos whined, and shot around the nearly comatose line of cars.

Somebody honked but a quick glance in the mirror showed the light only now turning red so who could be mad at me for doing what they were afraid of doing? Besides, they didn't have some mysterious package hidden in their trunk needing to be delivered to some shadowy person at an oddly specific time.

Taking one highway to the next I made my way swiftly out of the city limits until arriving at a bar lit up by a neon sign that blinked and buzzed. The gas station next to it was little more than a stopover for truckers, weary travelers, and local teens with nowhere better to be.

I quickly reversed into a parking lot fronting the bar, checking out the vehicles around me. There weren't many but I wanted to know if anyone was posted up trying to look inconspicuous. Anyone could be hiding anywhere, true, but my first priority was if and where they could give chase.

Nothing suspicious set off my radar.

I had no clue what I was running but that was a part of the risk and the job description. And asking questions? Highly frowned upon. This was neither Fed

Ex nor UPS. I dialed a number on the throwaway in my cup holder and a woman answered. We went through a little two step before she told me to head into the bar.

That was the last place I wanted to be. I hated bars and clubs as a rule now. They brought back bad memories I'd rather leave behind. But I took a deep breath, grabbed my purse, and headed inside.

The inside was dark, dank and nearly empty even at this late hour. The bartender leaned against the bar, bored as she cleaned a beer mug and watched a sports channel with glassy eyes.

A group of four guys sat at a table in a corner talking low amongst themselves while one guy sat on a stool at the bar. I grabbed a stool at the far end and ordered a Jack and Coke sans Jack.

I'd been told to wait until someone contacted me. I didn't expect it to be one of the guys from the table nor did I expect him to be an asshole. Suppose I should've.

"What's up baby?"

The bartender disappeared as two of his friends walked up, trapping me in a triangle. I sat my ground, focusing on the proud face before me. He tried looming from six feet or so but I maintained my composure. His dark blue eyes said he was used to intimidating people.

"I believe the bartender left because I'm not your baby," I said as I slid my hand into my purse.

He made me uneasy in a way that had my radar blaring. I'd dealt with assholes like him before and it was never fun.

"Now I can't be sure about that. You're in my bar with your ass hanging off my favorite stool; it even has my name on it."

I was dumb enough to get up and look and he grabbed a handful of my butt. Before he could blink I spun and grabbed his nuts while pulling my 9mm out of my purse and jamming it against his privates. I hated being touch by strangers, but I especially hated having my butt grabbed by them. His eyes bugged in surprise, darting towards his friends.

"Crazy bitch-" One began.

"I wouldn't guys, my finger might slip."

The bartender returned with a matronly woman in a jump suit with a blue sapphire sparkling in her ear. She clapped theatrically as she smiled.

"I see you're a woman of exceptional standards but can you please leave Hamilton his jewels? I doubt he'd be any good as a eunuch."

"They worked fine for ancient civilizations."

"True, but we aren't so barbaric and I'd really like grandkids one day."

"Hmm, I don't know, he grabbed me without my permission." It was all I could do to keep my voice from breaking as old memories washed over me.

"I'm sure he's sorry; aren't you Hamilton?"

"Yes, ma'am."

"You should be telling her not me."

"I apologize for putting my hands on you."

I released him and retrieved my purse, glancing at the stool as I did sure enough there was his name. His mother guided me outside; I was thankful for the brisk winter air as we went to my car and concluded our business.

She scribbled a name on my proffered clipboard I was sure wouldn't register anywhere if we were even checking. I hopped into my baby and fought off a tremble, trying not to let the past overwhelm me as I took several deep breaths. Getting over past pain was still a work in progress which worked sometimes and didn't at others.

I started my car, shifted gears, and got out of there.

The phone got tossed out the window in pieces before I called my boss to let him know I was ok and successful. E took it enigmatically as always as if he expected nothing less.

Hanging up I headed home.

XX

My alarm buzz buzz buzzed its persistently irritating wack-up call. I slapped a hand down, poked my index finger on a tack, and cursed. Why had I fallen asleep with a bunch of tacks sitting around on the bedside table? Because I'd fallen asleep after hanging up posters of sexy half naked men. Duh.

I re-aimed for the clock which isn't supposed to go off on Sunday. With my finger in my mouth, I came to a miserable conclusion; it isn't Sunday.

Great, just another manic Monday honey.

I groaned, since when did I start saying "honey?" Geez, I must be getting old; my mom says honey.

Yoshi, the one reassurance in my getting-old-life, put her head under my free hand. I scratched her ears absentmindedly. My black velvet cat's purr could've woken up anyone near... had anyone been near.

I've always had affection for Super Mario and always considered the blue Yoshi a girl. I'd sit there trying not to lose her while my mom hollered in Spanish, "Meghan Wahlin, sitting so close will ruin your eyes." Here I am, still addicted to video games with above average eyesight. Waddaya know.

"One thing's for sure, Yoshi," I began as she stretched in her spot on our queen sized bed. "If I can't depend on men I can depend on you."

Taking Yoshi's lead I did my own stretch. Elbow propped on one knee I pushed against it until hearing, and feeling for sure, the satisfying pop in my spine. This groan was one of pure pleasure.

"Nothing like a morning stretch."

Yoshi meowed at me.

"I probably shouldn't stretch like that," I told her. "I'll be your age one day with arthritis, barely able to stand up straight like Quasimodo's wife. So what should two ladies eat for breakfast?"

She looked at me with her wild brown eyes. Meow.

"Good choice."

In all honesty I'm not old. Just 20 something going on forever, not too shabby if you ask me. At least I could stand and admire my 5' 8" frame in a full length mirror for more than a fleeting glance. No bags under my gray-blue eyes waiting to be packed for a red eye flight. My heavy chest was still winning the fight against gravity and even my tummy, a little...pleasant, was resisting the urge to hang over my waistband.

I smiled. Then frowned at my first major setback.

Here I am at 20 something years young, I deliberately tell myself, with braces. My dentists had tricked me. Oh yeah, corrective surgery will fix that gap right up. Sure, I believed that hype, who wouldn't? Now here I am three years later still shelling out payments for braces they swore I wouldn't need. Guess the means justifies the end.

That, at least, would end. It was my other evil which I dreaded. My mom had cursed me with a backyard big enough to build a mall on. A contractor could put the Mall of America on one lobe and two Hiltons on the other and still have room for parking. Geez. It seemed no matter how many times I worked out with my fitness instructor there was no erasing my ... inheritance.

Alright, maybe you think I'm overdramatizing.

I'm not.

I learned a few years ago that a cup could be placed on my butt without me even noticing. My ex, Thomas, thought it'd be funny to prove how fat I am, and not in the sense with a P.H. So there I was ironing, minding my own business, when Thomas gave me a hug "just because." Right. I went to pet Yoshi and spilled water all over us. Thomas fell out laughing while we glared a hole through him.

"See," he wheezed, "I told you. Damn thing's so big you don't even notice 16 ounces!"

Needless to say I kicked him out of my house and finally out of my life. That taught me a lesson, only date men who appreciated my curse. The only problem is that Eagan, Minnesota isn't exactly a black man haven although I always manage to get their attention no matter where I go. My neck rolling friend Carmen says;

"Girl, don't you know, brothers worship ass? Those Romans ain't shit with their goddess of beauty. Girl, please! Brothers worship the goddess of booty!" Then she'd laugh raucously.

Had I not grown up in a suburban neighborhood and, thus been teased all my life it might've made the transition easier. Unfortunately, my luck with men is no luck at all. It seems like if they aren't shot and killed then they were shooting and killing. A lose-lose for me especially considering my mistrust of most men in the first place.

"Oh well," I sighed, making my way into my kitchen which is black and chrome with more buttons than a spaceship command center. Yoshi waited for me while I was planning out...

"What's up bubble gum panties!"

I spun in a panic ready to fight.

Carmen was tickled by that apparently. "Girl, please, you ain't finsta whoop nobody naked." She laughed. "If I was a man I wouldn't even fight you; we'd be wrestling."

I'm not exactly a morning person but Carmen? Well, she's up bright and early no matter the time or day.

"You scared me half to death. I thought you were on a run."

That's how we paid our bills; making deliveries Fed Ex and UPS wouldn't dream of. Shoot, they wouldn't dare take such risks and truthfully, while I did make deliveries, I tried my damnedest to stay away from runs that'd put me behind bars: unlike Carmen who loved the risks and adrenaline.

"I finished early." Her smile was smug and full of...something that made me cover what little I could without blushing. Hey, it's all about the effort right?

"Girl, please," she scoffed. "I know what kind of product you're advertising; I just haven't been able to buy." Ended with a pout.

Since I hate living alone I opted to share a duplex with her. Of course, things're simple when your besty is your land lord. We get along fabulously, our main difference being our taste in men. Carmen didn't have much of a taste at all usually.

Carmen stands 5' 11" barefoot but her curves fit her confidence and runway strut. Plus, she has more attitude than I have booty, a trait she claims redbones in the hood tend to learn at an early age.

I take her sandy-brown haired, which she wears well past her butt, word for it. There's a patch of freckles over the perfect nose that set off her light green eyes. Carmen doesn't wear braces on her perfectly straight, sparkling teeth either. So, yeah, she's got me beat, even down to those pouty lips with that gentle crescent in the middle of the top one.

My Alan Jackson ring-tone told me it's 5 o'clock somewhere, reminding me that I had a job to do.

"I'm going to get dressed," I said, taking my food with me.

"You do that bubblegum panties."

CH2

"Eric has an emergency delivery." I called out to Carmen as I brushed out my shoulder length blond locks.

"Want me to roll with you?" she called back. "I'm still on the clock."

"Sneaky devil."

I made my way back to her. She sat on my navy blue suede couch. My living room is dark yet rich with a red, black, and blue décor all in their deepest forms like colorful secrets. I like the dark mixture, especially when the lights are low; it's like a velvet cave when I'm playing video games.

Carmen grinned at me. "I thought you knew the devil wears Prada."

The truth if I ever heard it. We both have good taste but where I'd wear Jordans and any heel I think is cute Carmen's fixated on high end everything. She's paid thousands for a pair of very cute heels that I thought weren't that cute. Mostly because I am to technology what Carmen is to fashion. She doesn't even know what kind of phone she has. To her it's a Sprint. Hilarious and adorable.

"Yes, sneaky devil, you can join me."

"Oh joy!" she laughed and clapped her hands.

After I was all bundled up to protect myself from this miserable Minnesota winter I went down to the garage to start my black Subaru Impreza. Beside him is my red Monte Carlo SS. I need to be able to maneuver while carrying different loads and unlike the Transporter things got real in the field and one suped up Audi wasn't going to cut it.

A text message brought me out of my reverie. Only one person would be texting me this early. It's not like there was a special ring tone or anything.

Martize is a part-time runner. He's also my current like interest, because love is too strong a word. He's sexy, charming and extremely well built, all 6' 1 inches of him. The best part is that the man is stable-hip hop hooray!-which is a ginormous plus in my book. He was also the first guy in a while I was drawn to who managed to earn more than a few minutes of conversation since I decided to rejoin the world after a traumatic experience a few years ago.

-Good morning, sexy, I'm thinking about you-

"Aww." Sigh.

-What are you thinking about?-

Wait for it. Aha!

-Meghan in a pair of heels, a skin tight skirt...my lips on her creamy thighs-

Made me blush, tightening low places I couldn't deal with all bundled up. What can I say? Lips on my thighs is my weakness and when those lips are skilled? Hmm, the thought alone made me shiver.

-Isn't it a bit early for such naughtiness?-

-I've been on the road all night, it's late for me-

-Where're you Martize?-

-On my way back from NY-

New York? Interesting but...

-I hope you can hold that thought until you return-

-You're asking a lot-

Made me chuckle

-Just think of how tasty I'll be-

-You're such a tease-

-Teasing's good for the sensual soul-

-I'll be there soon enough. Keep it juicy for me-

-I'll think about it-

-Later tease-

Now my morning felt a lot better.

XX

"Don't you look like the cat that ate Tweety bird." Carmen said when I reentered the kitchen.

"I just spoke to Martize." Why not be happy while it lasted?

"Go figure." She stuck out her tongue as if she'd just swallowed an oyster: We hated oysters.

For whatever reason she didn't like Martize, since the day they met she'd said he rubbed her the wrong way. Usually that'd mean he was trying to talk to her behind my back like dogs are wont to do. Most men had a bad problem of wanting Carmen over me which taught me a few valuable lessons. So if she feels Mr. Right Now is wrong I tend to keep her opinion in

mind. But I thought she was wrong about him since by her own admission he hadn't so much as tried to flirt with her.

"Meghan, it's time for new boots." A nice change of topic.

Incredulous, I replied. "These're brand new." And cute as hell, pink, my favorite color, Timberland heels.

"I mean a new style, every winter it's Timbs."

"Who made you the fashion police, Joan Rivers?"

"Girl, please, she's funny and all but if I was the FPD your ass would be under the jail, and that's a whoooole lotta ass to stuff under Shakopee."

I rolled my eyes. "Whatever, let's find out what this emergency run is."

XX

My adrenaline was racing from the speed I coaxed from my baby.

There's something about pushing the limits that gets my blood rushing. Feeling an engine redline, screaming to be shifted into a higher gear but leaving it at the edge until it was at that perfect spot? Then popping the clutch and riding out the powerful thrust... Hmm.

"I love this song!" Carmen exclaimed as Miranda Lambert sang about loading her shotgun-with a lit cigarette!-waiting on her abusive ex.

Carmen's all about righteous girl power. Surprisingly she now enjoys country music to an extent, although you probably wouldn't catch her listening to old school Conway Twitty or Randy Travis.

"So how'd you manage to finish your run early?"

She pointedly ignored me as Carrie Underwood began belting about digging the key into the side of his pretty little suped up four wheel drive. I thought carving a name into a leather seat was not only blasphemy but a sure fire way to end up under somebody's jail.

We pulled into the library parking lot where I rented all my books. I pulled a book from the seat pouch behind me then threw it onto Carmen's lap.

"What's this?"

"A book," I said dryly.

"Smart ass."

"Rather be a smart ass than a dumb ass."

"You're right; it's probably big enough to have a mind of its own."

"You should talk." I frowned.

"Girl, please, my ass isn't nearly as big as yours. You get three inches taller when you sit!"

She laughed as I stuck my tongue out at her. She pulled on a pair of white leather gloves with fur edges that matched her boots and coat then, without another word, she stepped out into a brisk, dreary day. Forecast actually said it might snow. Yeah.

XX

No questions asked, or Naq for short, is a small business in a small building on White Bear Ave which shares space with a barbershop. Eric owns the place and only kept the office for "filing" purposes.

The shop is what most would expect; hardwood floors, a big front window filled with different advertisements, barber chairs and the ubiquitous barbers and clients. I stood between two rows of black and silver adjustable chairs. All twelve were occupied, some turned towards the mirrors hanging behind each station and others turned towards one of the two suspended TVs.

Everything stopped when Motown started singing.

"I think my heart just broke..."

He's 6'3 and skinny with sharply tapered 360 degree brush waves. He has an oval shaped face filled by a large nose and lips too sensual for a man. He's handsome enough but I would never date one of Eric's friends. He's a masseur and can sing the panties right off a Catholic nun...and he knew it. He's from Detroit, thus the name, thus the swagger.

"Who let that angel out of heaven...?" he crooned.

He held his audience captive. His soulful brown eyes captured my grays in an unfathomably liquid lock. He snapped his fingers, moving towards me slowly until he stood barely half a foot away. I have a man but a woman would have to be deaf not to be at least a little...excited.

"You ain't gotta say a word naw..." Sent chills down my spine. Where'd he get the wind to stretch "naw" until it was nearly lost to his powerful melody?" Cause that look in your eyes says it all..."

Then he had the temerity to send his smooth tenor to soprano... falsetto... damn. How did a man's voice go so sweetly high?

"The question is," he sang quietly, a twinkle in his eyes. I could smell his subtle spicy cologne he was so close. "When you'll give in and let me call."

I smiled, patting his dimpled cheek. He'd been asking me out for more than a year, and while I admired his tenacity he was one of Eric's friends. I couldn't deal with any more drug dealers, gang bangers, or players. They were bad for my blood pressure. Besides, I'd seen some of the women Motown kept around, he wasn't hurting for female attention.

"When I finish thinking about it."

"Oh!" the entire shop instigated. They started ribbing him, bringing back a mellow atmosphere. He put his hands up, everyone listened.

"At least I can say she's thinking about it; that's a lot more than any of ya'll can say."

They laughed good-naturedly. He had a point there.

I'm known as hard to get, I'm not impossible I just have old fashioned views on dating. Can a man take me to dinner and a movie without trying to turn me into dinner while making a movie? Why can't men understand that sex is a relationship perk?

That aside, Motown has a reputation as being a romantic; he showed women respect, even hoes that didn't get it from other men and a good time. But he's Eric's homeboy and my best friend Alicia's surrogate brother. The latter made him awesome the former off limits.

I opened my coat and asked, "Where's Eric?"

"In his office," Motown told me. "Let me take your coat."

"No thanks, I'm not staying."

I walked through, ignoring hungry, creepy leers. Instead of finding Eric I nearly ran into his wife, Alicia.

"What's up fam of mine." She greeted happily, hugging me.

Alicia is model beautiful. Cocoa butter skin, direct dark eyes and perfect cheeks atop a perfectly proportioned 5'8" frame with Halle Berry curves. She wore brown thigh high boots over dark pants and a matching shirt that her straight black hair flowed over effortlessly.

"What's up?" I asked.

"Carmen should have your package." Shook me up a little. She saw my confusion and my hesitance and read both in a heartbeat. "She got paid for an advanced run because she deserves it, don't let her fool you."

I did feel foolish. Sneaky devil.

"Anyway, fam, your contact is Marcus Jacobs," her face twisted with an eye roll as she slid me a sticky note with an address. "Your fee has been doubled, take Motown with you."

Eric chose that moment to enter his office telling someone on the phone, "It's on the freeway right now."

Alicia rolled her eyes again. She told me once that they were having dinner when a smoker called him. She was far from happy but his money-over-broads mentality paid for all her fancy stuff. Ironic logic. Of course she didn't want him to leave so until their date was done he told multiple smokers he was "on the freeway."

I suppose hard habits die hard.

"What's up E?" I greeted.

He looked up. He has a short frame with wide shoulders and big biceps, but he wasn't what one would call stocky. He had enigmatic eyes and a habitual tendency of biting his nails way past the quick.

"What's up? I've got an irate businessman waiting on a package 30 minutes late." His voice told me he was hardly upset. He'd been making deliveries this way for years.

What did he deliver?

Ask me no questions I'll tell you no lies. Personally I didn't make self-incriminating worthy runs. What others did was none of my business.

I turned back to Alicia curiously. "So why would I need Motown's help?"

E spoke over his shoulder as he patted Alicia on her butt on his way past. "Town has never let me down."

"You say that like you trust him with your life."

Stopping in the doorway to his office he smiled, enigmatic as ever. "He has never let me down."

A simple yet profound statement.

XX

Motown has a small massage therapy business in the brick building behind E's; he calls it Mobile Masseuse because wherever you were in Minnesota he'd come to you. Apparently that was a service a lot of people were fond of. Alicia says he does hella well. I believe that because he drives a twin turbo Scion. It takes funds and knowledge to customize one car let alone a few and I knew from experience that he had a few vehicles.

I stepped outside into the frigid morning air and stopped short of leaving the doorframe because there was a man in a white ski mask at the end of the alley. He was heading in my direction but I chose to dismiss him and the bad vibes I suddenly started feeling because his head was buried in his phone deeper than an ostrich in quicksand.

I stepped to Motown's Scion and walked around it, enjoying the view. It has sky blue lighting stripes over a navy blue paint. The body kit is amazing; hood scoop, flared runners, spoiler and all.

The bad vibes I'd felt earlier suddenly intensified when pain and light exploded in my head, dropping me to my knees. Booted feet appeared in my peripheral but before I could reorient myself a heavy blow landed in my stomach, banging me against Motown's car, making it hard to breath.

His car alarm went off seconds before someone snatched me up by my hair, slapping me sideways.

"Leave this run alone, bitch." He growled into my ear.

"Hey!" Sounded like Motown to the rescue.

The man let me go. I looked up and there was Motown, lashing out with a straight kick that sent dude sliding on his back in the muddy snow. He rolled backwards before coming back to his feet, suddenly brandishing a gun.

He never got a chance to aim.

Motown spun with lightning fast reflexes; it was uncanny, he lashed out at the gun with one foot then, even on the slick pavement, continued his spin and jumped out of nowhere, rising horizontally, spinning a foot into my attacker's ear. Dude cried out, stumbled, and ran off with a dizzyish wobble.

For a second I thought Motown would chase him but he turned back to me. I must've been hella dizzy because I swear Motown was half naked with smoke rising off of muscles better defined as chiseled than skinny.

He picked me up as if I weighed nothing, without a word, carrying me back to his office. We ended up in his parlor, with its soft blue décor, where he laid me on a long soft couch.

"What hurts Meghan?"

He carefully took my coat off. I was glad he didn't ask if I was alright, I was so apparently not.

"My head hurts a little. He kicked me but my coat took most of the impact." Thank God for goose-down and layers.

He slid his hand under those layers as if we were that close. I was so shocked all I could do was gasp. His hands should've been cold but they were nimble, firm, and hot. So hot I may have bitten my lip, thankfully he couldn't see my face even if he was only being professional.

The layers didn't seem to exist for him as he ran a practiced hand over my ribs; his touch damn soothing, more so than I'd admit aloud.

Then it was over.

"Your ribs are fine; let me check your head."

I laid there under his ministrations, surprised that he was so gentle and competent. I got another surprise when I noticed what we were listening to; Five Finger Death Punch. Maybe I'm being narrow minded but how often does one find a black thug from Detroit listening to rock?

I have no clue what he did, some twisty-pressure-massage thing that not only felt amazing but did wonders for my head.

"Thank you, Motown."

His tone was light but his stare penetrating when he replied, "No problem, Meghan."

I tried so desperately to ignore his muscles but they had a slight sheen to them that drew the eye. Thankfully he rose and walked away.

"Why are you half naked, Motown?"

"I was exercising," he said as he returned with a multicolored pressed dress shiyou rt that clashed with his dark gray slacks and Havana Joe boots in a fashionable sense.

Carmen insists that I should carry a handgun, she's knows my dad trained me to use them but I usually only carry my ten shot Glock 17 in my purse. She liked guns for their power; I just like knowing I was much safer... if I didn't get attacked from behind. Motown slid into a belt holster with a Colt resting at the small of his back. He went to a hidden closet, I guess he trusted me because he typed a code in while I sat there, pulled out a black Pelle Pelle and a black turtleneck.

He donned both, patted himself in a few different places, nodded to himself in satisfaction then fixed a Bluetooth to his ear. After pulling on leather gloves he turned off some lights, flipped a "call my cell" sign and asked if I was ready while holding open the door.

A brisk breeze made me shiver.

"Someone just walked over my grave," I whispered, looking around the empty alley.

"Naw, you're with me, you'll be alright."

The feeling persisted. I locked eyes with him and saw nothing but earnest conviction.

"Seguro?" I asked.

"Yeah, I'm sure."

"No promesas?" I teased, trying to cheer myself up.

"You want a promise?" His voice serious.

Eric said he'd never been let down by Motown. High praise coming from him. That meant Motown went through all of E's bullshit and still came out on the other end.

"No, te tengo confiaza." If Eric and Alicia trusted him I could too, besides, hadn't he just saved me? This was the first time we were working together alone even though we had hung out over the past few years, still I had never given thought to trusting him.

We zipped over to find Carmen outside the library macking on some chick. I blew my horn, she looked up, waved, and continued her conversation. I could practically hear what she was saying in my mind. Something so slick the chick wouldn't be able to process it until two days later. They traded numbers, Carmen came to the car and, as a coup de grace, blew her a kiss. They'd probably had a talk with Carmen saying, "Girl, that's just my buddy."

"So why is Motown stuck on your bumper?" she asked, putting a small suitcase in my backseat.

"He's not." I smiled as he pulled ahead of us, blowing his horn.

He led us through a myriad of backstreets to a townhouse in Oakdale where he zipped into an alley without using his breaks. Damn good driving for a masseuse.

"Pretty good driving for a masseuse," Carmen pointed out.

I almost laughed, great minds and all that. "He's alright."

His garage popped open before he reached it. With NASCAR speed he jumped into a black Trail

Blazer. Before I knew it Carmen jumped out of my car and into his truck. Almost instantly enough bass to wake up the dead poured from it.

Guess she was tired of my company. Traitor.

CH3

We were being followed.

By a cop.

The Crown Victoria was so obvious when I began paying attention to my surroundings. Truth be told, being attacked and threatened first thing in the morning was so not my cup of cappuccino. With all that having gone down it was no surprise that my mind was occupied.

This entire run was starting to feel wrong.

We weren't supposed to ask questions, weren't supposed to open the package a la The Transporter but we weren't ex special forces, or spies who could jump over buildings and fight off 17 people at once. I could fight, I could shoot, but, truthfully, when push came to shove I would run my phat ass away from most danger given half the opportunity.

Flicking on my blinker I turned down a side street, hoping to get the cop off my ass. He hit his lights. I cursed as I pulled to the curb in front of some stranger's brown and white home with its manicured lawn. Motown parked about two houses behind us.

"Step out of the vehicle with your hands up!" The cop said over a loud speaker.

"What!" I gasped.

He repeated the message. I got it but I didn't get it. What the hell had I done? Without much choice I opened my door and stepped out, noticing, as he told me to keep my hands up and back to him, that I had two barrels pointed my way.

Suddenly Motown's Trail Blazer screamed as he pulled off. I looked back, eyes wide. I had a split panicky second to wonder if he was leaving me before the truth dawned on me. His truck veered straight for the cruiser. The cops realized it almost too late. They dived away as his black bumper guard crunched into the side of their cruiser, caving it in.

My eyes went wide.

Motown never stopped, just pushed it up over the curve, turning it onto its side. He waved frantically at me as he backed away. I was too shocked to move until gunshots rang out. Automatic rat-a-tats sent cracking ricochets flying off of Motown's armored body before I dived back to the safety of my own vehicle. He flew past me.

I wasn't far behind. Fuck that! I couldn't believe this mess. How hard could a run from one city to another be? This was turning into a cluster fuck.

"Motown," I yelled into my phone after it rang twice. "What the hell was that?"

"Those weren't police." His mellow voice was calm. Soothing.

"Huh?"

"Last time I checked, patrol officers don't have laser sights-"

"Maybe-" I started but the next words froze the blood in my veins.

"Or assault rifles."

"Not routinely girl!" Carmen added. "That's exclusive shit."

"I don't know who they were but something had them distracted, Meghan." Motown said.

"Distracted how?"

"Girl, you had your back to them!"

"Carmen what are you talking-" I shut up, knowing she was joking before I understood.

Oh.

XX

Motel 6.

Motown thought it prudent that we tried figuring out what was going on.

"You've been assaulted, threatened, and shot at," he said as he rubbed Carmen's shoulders. She sat with her eyes closed, purring louder than Yoshi. I couldn't tell whether he was rubbing her shoulders to relax her or himself.

I paced past them sitting on the queen sized bed and couldn't help but think the pronoun should be "we" but whatever. I didn't answer him because my phone rang.

"Hi, Martize." Made Motown look at me funny.

He didn't care for Martize any more than Carmen did. I couldn't say why because they didn't run in the same circles or deal with the same people. Even though I was supposed to trust Motown, and I was beginning to, Martize was my man and deserved my loyalty. I turned my back on them.

"I'm back in town, can I see you?" Martize asked.

"Maybe later, I'm a little bit busy right now."

"I wish you would stop pacing, Meghan, you're distracting me," Motown said just loud enough for Martize to hear. Carmen found that funny and gave him a high five.

"Who is that?" Martize demanded on cue.

"Just a few coworkers," I glared at them.

"Bet that, I'll call you back later."

He hung up before I could reply so I took my irritation out on Motown.

"Why would you do that?"

"Do what?" he asked, feigning innocence.

"You know what. You spoke up just loud enough for Martize to hear you."

He shrugged nonchalantly. "You should be giving thought to your current predicament."

"What do you think I'm trying to do?" I said angrily.

"It looks like you're yelling about speaking too loud that your man hears," Carmen said with an eye roll.

"We need to get out of here and finish this run. I'm here to help but I don't think you should keep using your Subaru."

"Why?"

"Someone apparently knows your car." He patted Carmen's shoulder then stood, walked to the window, peeped out. "I don't like how someone knew you were going on a run in the first place."

"Who would know that besides E and Alicia?" I asked.

"Isn't it obvious?" he shot back, waiting on me to answer.

"Whoever commissioned the run," I said after a moment. "Or someone close to that person."

"So the best thing for us to do is be careful as we deliver this to its destination."

I shrugged. "Well let's go."

My phone rang as we put on our coats. I frowned when I checked my caller ID and saw that the number was blocked. I didn't like blocked numbers; if I was important enough for you to call then I should be important enough to know who the hell you are when you do.

I ignored it as I followed Motown and Carmen to the door.

Snow fell lightly as Motown stopped in front of the open door and held out his leather gloved hand.

"You'll drive my car for the rest of this run," he said when I looked at him curiously.

"Yes boss," I replied dryly, dropping the keys into his hand.

Motown suddenly cursed and slammed the door. "We gotta go." Before I knew it he was barricading the door with a short dark dresser.

Headlights flashed across the bedroom window as Motown waved us to the only escape route we could take: a window that led to a rickety looking fire escape. He pushed it open as far as it would go. Apparently the damn thing wasn't up to code: it only went up half way.

"We'll never make it through there," Carmen said.

"It's this way," he pointed at the window, "or that way where more fake cops are coming."

We all followed his finger to the door. Carmen shook her head, stepping to the window, kicked it up another few inches then shimmied her way through, growling at Motown about buying her new leather.

Car doors slammed as I began to climb. Carmen pulled my arms, desperation in her voice.

"I hear them out back." Tug tug.

Halfway through the window someone or something banged against the bedroom door.

The stupid window chose that moment to crash into the small of my back.

"I'm stuck!" I cried, wiggling.

I felt Motown straddle me as more banging occurred and Carmen continued to tug. Given the situation I should've been able to ignore his proximity but that was harder said than done with his package pressed against my mailbox. He pressed down against me as he pushed at the window and it abruptly screeched open just enough for me to squeeze through. I flopped down on the snowy landing at Carmen's feet.

She screamed for Motown. I turned, catching the end motion of the bedroom door crashing open. He dove behind the bed as gunshots reverberated through the room. Carmen shot through the window, glass exploded everywhere.

"Meghan get to the car."

I hated leaving but I knew one of us had to get a vehicle up and running or we'd be stuck worse than a newb playing a level three boss. I went as fast as the ladder would let me go event hough it felt as though it would separate from the wall at any given moment.

Some guy in all black was trying to force his way into my car. A shot rang out and he lurched aside with a strained holler.

"Go, Meghan, go," Carmen shouted.

I went, not even daring to look back. I tried to get the door open with the keys I had before remembering that I had switched keys with Motown. I ran around to his truck. Before jumping in I caught a glimpse of him and Carmen running down the fire escape. A movement in my peripheral caused me to spin around. Only the turn helped me miss the butt stock of a rifle aimed at my belly. It glanced off as I struck with an elbow to his nose. He staggered back. A shot rang out and he crumbled.

"Meghan," Carmen quipped. "This ain't the time to be dancing."

Her eyes glowed with excitement as her panted breath steamed the air between us.

I looked down at the dead guy and cringed, wondering who he might have been in life. Motown pulled up his mask and took a photo with his phone then said:

"Let's just finish this run: it's giving me a headache."

CH4

"How can you be so cavalier right now ya'll just killed people," I asked, trying not to hyperventilate.

I stood there staring between the pair and the body incredulously. Carmen looked like she either just had an orgasm or was about to while Motown looked implacable. I didn't realize I was shaking until Motown gently pulled the keys from my hand.

"Carmen, go get the package out of her car," he ordered as he guided me to the back seat.

"I'll call my home boy and have him tow her car to his garage."

"What? Why?" I managed to say. Then I turned around to get a better look at my car and saw the tires had been slashed. Now that pissed me off. "They slashed my tires? I just bought those tires."

"Girl, tires are the least of your worries," Carmen said after returning with the suitcase sized package.

Motown called E on speaker phone as he drove.

"Hello?"

"Why am I being shot at on a run, E?" I shouted.

"Motown what is she talking about?"

"Let me tell you what I'm talking about," I said angrily before explaining the situation.

"Listen, Meghan, you signed on to do a job, no one was aware that it would be such a hassle and yet the best thing, the only thing, to do is just finish the run and get it over with. I'll call you back in a minute with what details I can, until then fall back and try to relax."

Without another word he hung up. No apology, no answers as to who might be after me or this package. Nada. I was beginning to regret taking this job in the first place.

Initially taking this job had been a blessing. I hadn't been able to find any decent work anywhere when Alicia told me E needed another delivery person. When he told me I got to choose my own hours, the pay was great, and that I didn't have to worry about answering to anyone except himself and Alicia I was hooked. Plus I got to work alone when I didn't feel like being bothered by another human being and maintain my anonymity.

Admittedly this was the first time in the year since I'd been working for E that something this dramatic has occurred. Most of the time the most trouble I have is somebody making unwanted advances or some disgruntled receiver of a package not wanting to accept delivery. I can deal with that. But my arrangement with E was that he wouldn't send me on potentially deadly or dangerous runs. Thinking back on that now, I realize he never made me any promises on the latter.

Still I was here and I had a job to do and by Lara Croft's panties I was going to do it.

Motown drove us to a little shop in Minneapolis that sold bubble tea. It was a peaceful little shop that offered a variety of bubble tea flavors. It wasn't the first time he'd taken me there so I ordered a large mango berry tea after he ordered a large strawberry kiwi for himself and Carmen.

Carmen found us a table where we could see through the wide front glass window and still be able to slip out the back door if something just happened to kick off. There was one student at a table on the other side of the shop on a laptop and a couple at another. I sat facing them with my back to the rear exit then tried to use the gelatinous mango bubbles as a welcome distraction. It didn't work.

Have I ever mentioned video games are like my chocolate, except they don't go straight to my thighs? Yea, well, they are. I pulled out my LG Envy and loaded a game.

"What are you playing," Motown asked leaning over the table.

"Street Fighter," I huffed not looking up at him.

"Ooh, somebody's feeling violent," Carmen piped up.

Before I could reply Motown's ringing phone drew all of our attention.

"It's E," he told us before answering. He listened for a second, adding the obligatory "rights" and "hmm hmms" as we waited, then hung up with a blank face.

"There's been a change to the run." He held up a hand, forestalling my objection. "Whoever commissioned the run used an alias that won't do us any good. We'll make a transfer drop over north then move on to Brooklyn Center to complete the run."

"Hopefully," Carmen said, "whoever is pulling this bullshit won't be aware of these changes."

"Hopefully," I said without much conviction.

For the third time today my phone rung with a private number. Again I ignored it.

"Maybe you should answer the next time your phone rings," Motown suggested. "It might be someone related to this run."

"No one related to this run should have my number."

"Maybe E gave it to them," Carmen shrugged.

"Eric wouldn't give my number out."

"My boy just texted me, he says he needs to see us at his shop pronto," Motown said.

So we took our tea over to JT's auto body and repair shop. It was less like a shop than an office building with a body shop attached to it. Most mechanic shops I'd been in were gritty and not so clean while JT's looked like a maid had just done her rounds.

JT was a rambunctious flirtatious man of about average height with four gold front teeth. He wore a denim jumpsuit that was too clean for a head mechanic. It didn't look like he ever got dirty. He literally hollered when he saw Motown.

"What up though, boi." He waved before shaking Motown's hand in some weird homeboy pattern. "Damn who are these beauties you got rolling with you, boi?"

"Meghan, Carmen, this is JT," he said by way of introduction.

"Well, I must say it sure is a pleasure to meet your acquaintance." He gave us the onceover so blatantly that I couldn't even begin to call it creepy.

"Boy, you ain't fine enough to be eating me up with your eyes", Carmen sassed.

"Woo! You got yourself a live one, boi," he laughed affably.

"Yea," Motown agreed, eyeing me, "they're cool peoples. So what do you have to show us?"

JT walked over to a desk with an Intel Qx6700 and three open screens. I looked at him in a new light, perhaps he wasn't just a mechanic after all.

"Well, when I was trading those shredded tires for some new ones I happened upon this little black box." He pointed to a cigarette sized box sitting next to his computer. "This little black box just so happens to be a tracking device."

He looked at us as if to say why would somebody be tracking you? No one said a word.

"Well, ya'll ain't gotta say nothing to me, but I'd be careful doing whatever it is you're doing. This ain't no corner store device. I'm jamming it now with this little faraday cage but ain't no telling who put it there."

"So what can we do about it?" I asked.

"Get into your suped up Subaru, take the box to a river and throw it in, or park somewhere and see who shows up." He shrugged. "Either way you can't leave it here."

We all understood the apparent danger of being tracked without a word being said.

"Can you block it somehow if we take it with us?" Carmen asked.

"When we take it with us," Motown interjected, earning a nod from JT.

OZ Random

"Right," Carmen sassed. "Can you jam it?"

My phone rang with another blocked number. I couldn't imagine it'd be more than one person calling me private in the same day.

"You do know it's impolite to call someone private right?" I growled by way of introduction.

"Sometimes privacy is a luxury we can't afford to lose Miss Wahlin," a deep male voice replied.

Considering the fact that one of the reasons I like this job is the anonymity I found his answer both rude and hypocritical.

"So you invade someone else's to preserve your own?" Anger tinged my voice.

I hate to think about it but some memories sting worse than a hidden nest of angry wasps.

When I was 17 I thought I was invincible, that I knew everything I needed to know about the world. That's until two jerks decided they wanted to take me home against my will. My mom did everything to keep my story in the spotlight so when I finally managed to escape it was a huge deal.

I find it ironic that I found myself needing to escape a second time; from the media, well wishers...everyone.

Needless to say I'm a little screwy when it comes to privacy.

Motown and Carmen motioned for me to put my phone on speaker. I did. The stranger's voice sent goose bumps down my arms. His voice, while deep and obviously cultivated, had a sinister tinge to it I could only describe as dark.

"We all do what we must," he said.

"So who are you and why are you calling me?"

"I'd like to take you on a date."

Every eyebrow rose in surprise.

"Huhn?"

"If you can 'huhn,' I'm confident you can hear."

"That doesn't make any sense," I mumbled to Motown in Spanish.

"Sure it does," Darkness replied in kind, surprising us again. "You have a package which belongs to me. I understand you're having... difficulties delivering it. I suggest we talk."

"You still haven't told me your name," I pointed out.

"I'm the man you need to know. Meet me at Club Sin at 10 o'clock and we can get better acquainted."

He hung up before I could reply. Who did he think he was? Arrogant, self-centered asshole.

"So are we going?" Carmen asked. "Club Sin is supposed to be all about skin and everything that most people are afraid to admit they do in the day of light."

"Why do you seem so excited?" I asked.

"Girl, it's twice as big as any club and so exclusive you can only get in by invite." Her green eyes positively glowed.

My phone buzzed a second after she finished speaking. The text invited me and three guests to enjoy a night in the club's VIP.

"That's a sure fire way to keep an eye on someone," Motown said.

"Who cares?" Carmen shrugged. "It's *Club Sin*."

I called Eric to see what he thought but besides confirming the caller who'd commissioned the run did, indeed, have a deep voice he didn't tell me anything other than;

"It's your run, figure it out."

I'd never been on a run this intense. I felt out of my element, reminded of things best left unremembered.

CH5

With not many options available, I made the not-like-I-had-another-choice decision to visit the club. It almost surprised me that the latest address we'd received from E was the same address JT found on his computer when he looked up Club Sin. I shrugged away the surprise considering how everything that shouldn't make sense did and everything that should make sense didn't.

JT handed me a heavy metal box with the tracking device inside.

"Well Beauty-of-the-Week I can't say it wasn't a pleasure being in your company. Next time maybe we can meet in better circumstances eh?"

"JT," Motown clapped him on the shoulder good naturedly. "We appreciate your help but she's spoken for."

He never said by whom but the predatory gleam in his eyes let me know exactly who he thought he was talking about. I chose to ignore him and directed my next question back to JT.

"Will this block the signal?"

"It will," he replied with a knowing smile. He checked his monitors and said, "I don't see any suspicious vehicles around the shop so ya'll should be good to go. Good luck."

"Good looking fam," Motown said as they did their homie handshake.

Snow was falling moderately when I pulled up next to Motown and Carmen, fat sticky flakes that promised to stick worse than a wet tongue on a frozen pole. Motown took us on a circuit to be sure we weren't being followed before heading towards the Mall of America where we would shop for new outfits that met Club Sin's strict dress code.

The snow did nothing to hamper Motown's speed or driving abilities. Slush spewed off his tires as he expertly wove through early day traffic. I could just imagine him shifting gears with the flow of an off road rally car racer while maintaining the awareness of someone who has been pulled over by the police a time or few because he even managed to slow us both down enough to cruise by a speed trap by swiftly downshifting before we could be clocked. I was impressed.

When we finally parked on the lower levels of the MOA's parking ramp Carmen jumped out with bright excited eyes.

"Damn, that man can drive!"

Said man took the parasitic tracker from my car. He ran over to the Metro Transit lot and caught a bus that was leaving; spoke to the driver for a second while surreptitiously putting the device in the bus's wheel well before swaggering back to us with a wicked grin. Now whoever was tracking us would be thrown off by following the bus.

"That should buy us some time." He wrapped an arm around both of our waists. "Now which one of you brilliant starlets is ready to be lavished by Motown's pocket book?"

In truth with everything that had happened this morning I would rather not do anything other than finish this run immediately. I knew that it was necessary to get into Club Sin but I couldn't figure out how they could be so nonchalant after the day we had.

"I hate clothes shopping," I groaned at the same time Carmen purred.

"Please stop impressing me before I'm forced to let you in these panties."

He laughed as he squeezed us lightly. "I don't make promises I can't keep."

I'd been to the MOA twice; once to celebrate Alicia and Eric's son's birthday at Camp Snoopy and another to drop off a package. Motown made it feel like a new world. He guided us around as if he owned the place. In fact, almost every store we entered he knew someone. A majority of who were women. When Carmen called him on it he gave that nonchalant shrug of his.

"When I first opened Mobile Masseuse I printed out 2000 business cards and spent all day walking around the mall introducing myself." He grinned ruefully. "I gave so many sample massages I had to pay myself for the time spent."

"Sample massages?" Carmen asked.

"Five minute shoulder and neck rubs," he explained. "When it was all said and done I got1276 cards back in a month, about half of which are still friendly if not clients," he finished proudly.

We walked into a high class beauty salon where Motown immediately dominated the room. We stopped at a soft pink marble counter while a dozen hi's, catcalls, and quite a few hugs and air kisses were showered on him. There were a few women under high-tech looking blue and silver hair driers, sitting comfortably in peach colored recliners as their feet were soaked in bubble spas and their nails attended to, and two others relaxing on overstuffed couches to our right. I expected him to start stripping or throwing money the way the working women gave him their attention.

"Girl," Carmen whispered in my ear, "you look sooo jealous right now."

Whatever. I spied a tall, elegantly dressed woman with dark auburn hair and scintillating blue eyes storm out a back office. Even with anger clouding her face and giving her runway strut all the more fierceness I'd be a liar if I said she wasn't absolutely mesmerizing.

"She's too beautiful for words," Carmen murmured to herself.

She stormed up to Motown flashing signs with her hands so fast I thought she might be casting a spell on him. In her heels she was four or five inches taller than him and I could tell from the bounce of her cleavage that her hefty boobs were real. It made me wonder why he wanted me when he could clearly have women like her. I was clearly Super Nintendo to her PlayStation 2: outclassed.

Motown signed back and just when I thought he'd forgotten about us he turned to address two stylists.

"Brittany, Annaise, are ya'll busy?"

"Not now," one answered as the other shook her red pixie cut.

"Meghan meet Brittany," he said brusquely pointing out the brunette with light gray eyes.

"Carmen, Annaise." He gave them instructions to fix us up for a "fancy extravaganza" we were attending that night. I protested but he gave me a look saying, "trust me it's just a little strawberry to your blond. You'll be radiant," in such a smooth baritone I couldn't help but acquiesce.

Motown guided his friend back to her office with a hand on her lower back. I caught a glimpse of her weeping onto his shoulder before I was pointedly spun around and engaged in conversation by Brittany.

XX

We'd spent three hours, three whole hours, shopping after the salon. I had no doubt that they were trying to distract me from the stress of the run. They were actually doing a good job in one regard but not in another. Motown was a gracious host, regaling us with funny stories, singing, and critiquing our outfits with a professional eye while Carmen played the perfect wing woman. Still, after the easy stuff; shoes, jewelry and clutches—he and Carmen agreed were essential to the perfect outfits—he caught my hesitance to buy clothes.

"What's the matter?" he'd asked as he stood behind me giving me a sample massage while happier-than-a-geek-with-her-first-ComiCon-lover Carmen was off trying on yet another ensemble.

"I hate shopping for clothes."

"Telling me why might make you feel better," he suggested gently.

"You wouldn't understand," I sighed, "you're a man."

"You'd be surprised how understanding I can be."

Carmen sauntered out of the dressing room in a slinky one shoulder tan printed dress that complimented her skin tone and fit better than matching puzzle pieces. I envied her ease to just grab something off the rack and slide right into it but not wanting to dampen her mood I smiled and told her how amazing she already knew she looked in yet another outfit.

Motown rubbed tension from my shoulder while saying, "I use to kick it with this older woman, D. She was a hearty woman with an expansive bust and ass. She took me shopping with her one day and I snapped on a girl who was giving her dirty looks while whispering to her friend.

"D asked me why I had snapped and laughed at me when I told her why." He sounded incredulous that she'd laughed at him. "She told me she'd been plus one her entire life and would never aspire to be as thin as a mannequin model because you know what God invented for women just like her?"

I answered belatedly once I realized it wasn't a rhetorical question. "What, a corset?"?

He snorted. "Nope, a tailor."

"A tailor," I repeated dryly.

"Hell yea," he chuckled. "I didn't enjoy shopping once upon a time either. Nothing ever fit right on my narrow ass. Something was either too long or too short, too baggy or too tight. I was always clean but I hated looking like I was drowning in someone else's brand-new hand me downs because we both know I'm not wearing no tight clothes."

That earned a smile.

"D put me up on game. Now I go into any store I see something I like and get it tailored.

"I say that to say this, Meghan. You're a naturally curvy woman, which I get can be frustrating at time, but you wouldn't even qualify as plus size. So the best thing to do is say fuck the mannequins, fuck the advertised stereotypes and take your shopping experience into your own hands.

"Are you with me?"

"I guess," I replied even though his understanding made me feel much better. I'd wondered why he'd forced me to buy clothes I otherwise wouldn't have.

He shook my shoulders playfully. "I said are you with me?"

"Yes, okay," I agreed more cheerfully with a small laugh, "I'm with you."

"Good, because there's somewhere I've been dying to take you."

He took me to a small Oriental shop. There were rows of fabric artfully taking up much of the front of the space, a long counter and three changing rooms to the back. There was a pleasant yet unidentifiable scent permeating the air that reminded me of a relaxing beach night for some reason.

After a few minutes of Motown talking to the proprietress I found myself draped in the most exquisite backless dress I'd ever seen. It was pearlescent, shimmering between white and rose petal pink whenever I moved. The hem flowed like a lacy petal torn sharply on one side which exposed my entire right thigh. It wrapped around my neck not unlike a bikini top for all the cleavage it showed but even without a bra it was supportive as if it had been customized with big breasts in mind.

"You look so radiant that if you were mine I'd kiss you until your knees buckled," Motown growled.

Motown's comment threw me off. I had to remind myself he was one of Eric's homeboys and I have a man. Kiss me until my knees buckled?

"Get outta here with that noise!" I wailed even though I felt heat race through me.

I felt beautiful standing there with my hair classically waved a la 1960's pin up; more strawberry than blond. I never wore much make-up but Brittany had brought out my eyes with a hint of eye shadow, gave me this ultra-sexy cat's eye, and added gloss to my lips so they glimmered like a pink sunrise.

The dress only amplified it all.

Mei, an older Japanese woman who swore Motown's hands were blessed by Buddha himself, asked him what shoes I'd wear. She called him Momo, was thin, matronly, and wore her jet black hair in one long braid.

He held up a bag with a pair of fancy heels Carmen would be proud of. They were almost as pink as my hair and lips. Open toes and heel, the covering for the bridge of my foot was cut out in shapes not unlike snowflakes you make with folded paper and scissors.

"You like?" Mei asked, eyeing me critically in the tall mirror.

"Yes," I replied, running my hands over the smooth fabric.

"Momo you pay, I finish, you pick up later."

Mei practically dragged me back to the changing room.

For a confusing second I thought she'd brought me back to the wrong room because every stitch of clothing I'd been wearing, except my Timberland heels, was gone. Replaced by clothes I knew weren't mine.

It reminded me of things I didn't want to remember, taking me back to a time when two assholes kept me locked away for their own private amusement.

"Motown," I hissed over the stall door in a growing panic as memories began to break through the dam I had built.

He swaggered over innocently as I stood there naked and afraid of memories that threatened to overwhelm me.

"Where are my clothes?"

He didn't do it out of spite I told myself. He doesn't know about your past. He isn't trying to control you.

But my heart raced.

My breathing grew ragged. Choppy.

"Meghan what's wrong?"

Sweat beaded over my hands and forehead.

"Please," I begged softly.

There wasn't enough air. It was suddenly too hot. The changing room too confining.

Motown didn't understand what was happening. He moved closer.

"Meghan?"

I backed away. "Please please please. Gimme back my clothes." The mirror behind me squeaked as I slid down into as small of a ball as I could. Tears broke free from my eyes.

Mei's shop faded away.

XX

"Their names were Ira and Derrick. They were cousins both 5'9" and brown skinned but Derrick was the heavier of the two with long braids that would make my skin crawl when they brushed over me while Ira kept his hair neat and short.

"They kept me in a windowless room 15' long, 8' wide, 10' high. At first I thought it was some kind of bunker or something. There was carpet, a bed, a stainless steel toilet and sink combo, and a door-less three corner shower open to the room. Mirrors and cameras that I couldn't break were at every angle. It turned out to just be a pervert's room in a pervert's house."

I shuddered as I took a deep breath, staring off into space. I wanted to live life, not relive a nightmare, and telling the story never got easier with repetition. As I told Motown and Carmen from the beginning, I didn't often have such intense reactions to most stimuli anymore; it's just that some things hit me harder than I expect: thankfully, they listened stoically.

"It was something they did without any outsiders knowing. They did what they wanted when they wanted. They held the power and never let me forget it. My defiance was not tolerated. They starved me, drugged me, beat me, steamed the room until I was redder than Knuckles or froze the room until I was bluer than Sonic, sometimes both in a matter of hours, for long periods of time.

"None of which unnerved me more than when they took my cloths."

It had taken Carmen and Mei close to 30 minutes to calm me down. Carmen said I'd screamed every time Motown came near me which made me feel terrible. Somewhere in my mind I'd assumed he was trying to be charming, playful even, by changing my clothes but come to find out some random girl had entered my dressing room and spilled soda all over my clothes then took it upon herself to replace them.

Motown hadn't even known but he shrugged off my apology and hugged me. He'd held me for a good while, whispering about safety and security in Spanish. Finally he asked what triggered my panic attack.

So we were sitting on a bench, me sandwiched between him and Carmen, as I told them about my kidnapping. He held my hand and every time I glanced into his soulful brown eyes they were always full of nothing more than compassion and anger. If I'd seen an ounce, a smidgen even, of pity I know he would never have heard my story.

"For whatever reason that became more significant to me than anything else. It wasn't the nudity or the rape or anything I was forced to do that got to me.

"It was the utter lack of choice." My voice broke even after all these years.

Carmen swore vehemently. She'd never heard this story either.

Clearing my throat I continued.

"I got use to their leers even when they made me do the most ridiculous things for their entertainment. If I disobeyed, though, or didn't do something to their standards I was stripped of whatever outfit or costume they deemed me fit for at any given moment."

"I believe clothes became a kind of shield. I knew they had all the power and control but when they snatched away my shields that left me feeling defenseless even though I wasn't; it was an insult to my dignity. I paused and, eyes closed, took a deep breath."

We sat in a long companionable silence I appreciated as we took in the sounds and sights of the mall; children laughing, random snippets of conversation as people walked by, vendors trying their pitches to sale their wares.

"It doesn't surprise me that the choice is a big deal to you," Motown said presently. "We all deal with fucked up situations in our own ways. But you know what?"

He turned squarely to me, admiration and pride shining in his eyes. I knew in that moment that no matter what he'd always have my back.

"What?" I asked nearly hypnotized by the strength behind his gaze.

"You were stronger than them both and brave enough to endure then escape. I can wholeheartedly say I'm proud to count you as my friend, Meghan."

"How did you escape?" Carmen asked before I could choke up a response.

"I pretended to fall for them and they began to believe it so they stopped shackling my feet and hands. Derrick liked when I was drugged and I knew it. One day he brought me out of the room sober and completely unfettered while Ira was out.

"He had this whole candle lit dinner set up with wine and everything. I saw my opportunity to switch glasses when he pulled me onto his lap for kisses. I thanked him profusely for being so sweet until his now drugged glass, and my pure wine, was empty. At the first sign of the drug kicking in I broke his nose, stomped his dick and drove a steak knife into his eye. More or less. Ira was later caught, convicted, then murdered in prison," I finished.

"Serves them bitches right," Carmen snarled.

It hadn't been that cut and dry but there wasn't much use dwelling on the rage I'd unleashed on them before they died.

"You know, we have about an hour left before Mei is done with your dress," Motown said as he stood and smiled. "How about we do something to lighten the mood?"

"What do you have in mind?" Carmen stood and stretched.

He grinned at me. "Video games."

I grinned back. "Oh joy."

Carmen groaned. "Can't I just do more shopping?"

CH6

Motown was full of surprises which delighted me and actually made me reevaluate his worth. Again.

As promised he took us to a small arcade on the top floor. It was a true gamer's arcade hosting about 30 games; none of which spit out tickets for prizes. I looked longingly at Soul Blade and Street Fighter vs. Capcom but they were as heavily occupied as Resident Evil and some of the more popular racing games.

After about a minute of Carmen grumping and grousing he gave her a prepaid debit card with $5000 on it with a smile. She squealed, hugged him, then planted a kiss right on his mouth which surprised us both before leaving us alone. Relatively speaking.

He grinned goofily then shrugged at me unapologetically.

"How can you afford to just give her five stacks?" I asked as $10 worth of quarters tinkled out of the gold change machine. He shrugged, handing me about half.

"I make more than enough to be generous sometimes."

"But you know she'll spend every cent-"

"And be all the happier for it," he said dismissively as he lead me towards Time Cops. "Besides it gives us time to talk one on one."

Either he knew I enjoyed first person shooters or he picked it because it had enough room for two. I couldn't tell but either way he won a few more brownie points. It didn't hurt that he actually knew how to play.

I'd known of Motown for about a year before I'd actually met him. He went to high school with Alicia and absolutely doted on her which she took as much advantage of as he allowed. Once he realized his white collar ways weren't going to win her away from her hustling boyfriend/son's father he settled down to love her like a sister.

One day they were hanging out and got caught up with some drugs. He took the case, fought it down to a lesser charge then did a year in Ramsey County's workhouse. Unbeknownst to anyone him and Eric met and clicked right away. Not until months later did they share family photos where Alicia was the prime suspect in some.

"Wait a minute you're the Motown I keep hearing about?"

"Wait a minute you're the E I keep hearing about?"

Or so the story goes. Either way they've been family ever since.

The two of us met at a family picnic on the 4th of July. I remember he'd been dressed in new Jordan's, a fresh button up, pressed slacks—with a belt!—and a fitted Detroit New Era. He's right, in retrospect everything did look like baggy hand me downs. I can honestly say he didn't impress me much.

Alicia had always complained about E's little homeboys. They were all either trying to get on, hang on, or play on E's reputation in her opinion. As we got older I came to realize that she doesn't see them as bosses of Eric's stature. Except Mike Mike and Motown who worked in their own ways, didn't request a handout, and subsequently grew into their own responsibilities.

Standing next to him now I had to admit that he wasn't like any of Eric's other little homeboys. I had to admit he surprised me and possibly intrigued me on a new level I had never considered. And in all honesty I had to admit I was kind of starting to like him. Oh joy, I so didn't need this.

"*Un peso para su piensas*?" he asked.

He gazed down at me speculatively as the game took us through a C.G. sequence we couldn't just skip through.

"You're like a level in a video game I can't quite figure out," I told him honestly.

"Perhaps," he chuckled with an affected British tone before returning his attention to the bad guys on the screen, "you should accept what's in front of you instead of trying to figure it Out"

"I don't put that much faith in religion."

"Have I done or told you anything wrong? Ever?"

I shot a few bad guys, inserted a quarter after "dying," and thought about it. He stayed quiet, and alive, I knew he was waiting. He wanted me to trust him but trusting anyone was hard for me.

The quick answer was no but I chose not to tell him that. Instead I smacked his arm.

"Alicia told me of a time you tried to look up my dress!"

He frowned thoughtfully then threw his head back to bark out a laugh. Then he gave his signature shrug, tossing in quarters to continue.

"Not quiiite true," he grinned, "I still remember that night. You were driving your red Monte Carlo back then."

"That was almost two years ago." He remembered that?

He shrugged. "Some moments are more memorable than others. You were wearing an amazing skintight yellow dress and gold bangles and Steve Madden six inch sandals. I thought you looked sexy and priceless. Your back was to us, I'd just pulled up and stood next to Sis and I swear I couldn't help but enjoy the view. Then you bent over. Straight legged. From the waist.

Gawd," he growled, shaking his head.

Ok, so I was flattered. He made it sound so...sexy. His growl was so primal and full ofbarely contained passion I bit my bottom lip.

"Your dress didn't rise high enough to actually show anything but the teasing thought that it could, at annny given second, rise and show all your nude goodies was enough to get a young sexually driven Motown sprung faster than T-Pain on a stripper."

"Alicia didn't guiiite tell it like that," I drawled matching his playful drawl.

We laughed and the tension eased a little.

"So is that the worse you could come up with to not put faith in me?"

We both died. In went more quarters.

"How about we see what happens."

"Talking about a level you can't figure out; what about you?"

"What about me?"

"Well your back story is odd if don't mind me saying so. Your mom dukes did missionary work in Mexico, viva la raza, and your pops is from England, long live the queen, but you were raised in Wisconsin.

I don't get how that adds up but let's just say I accept that. Cool.

"I also accept that you decided to finish school from home after your fiasco with whats their-nuts. What I can't quite figure out is why you work for E instead of for some multibillion dollar gaming company like you've always dreamed of?"

I gaped at him. "How did you even know that!" I'd never told him about my dad, who'd died of a heart attack when I was 13, or my interest in game design.

"It's called active listening. I listen even harder when I like someone."

Carmen darted though the arcade's double glass doors, bags waving on her arms like haphazardly placed feathers.

"You won't believe..." she panted, "who I just saw."

"Who?" we asked simultaneously, instantly alert. Game forgotten.

"Martize."

"My Martize?" I squeaked embarrassingly.

"Naw," Carmen rolled her eyes. "Old McDonald's Martize e-i-e-I duh."

"Have you called or texted telling him where we'd be?" Motown asked.

"We left our phones in the lockers when-" I stopped when he held up a hand.

"I'm asking you a very simple and important question, Meghan." His entire demeanor had changed. He'd gone from easy going charm to direct and commanding faster than a computer calculates the square root of 69.

"No." I felt a little defensive.

"I knew I didn't trust his ass."

"He could just be chilling or shopping you know."

Neither looked like they were buying that.

"Was he alone?" Motown asked Carmen.

"No, he was with a bunch of dudes."

"See-" I began but their deadpan faces made me stop.

"There aren't many chances of happenstances," Motown said.

"So do we avoid him and slip out?" Carmen asked him. "Or do we confront him?"

Since I faced them I saw between their shoulders when two walnut toned black dudes with big necked wrestling frames scanned the arcade and spotted me. Recognition flared in their eyes a moment before they tapped Martize. Our eyes met.

"It's too late," I told them, "they already found us."

On the game's screen there was a countdown to continue ticking.

I found that kind of ominous.

Martize wore a form fitting black turtle neck, dark denim jeans and black Air Max's. His three "friends" wore unrelieved black from chest to boots.

Maybe Motown and Carmen's suspicions were rubbing off because while Martize gave me a brittle half smile his friends were all business-like which seemed incongruous.

"Hey baby doll," he greeted with a soft kiss.

He rubbed my ass, holding me close, while locking eyes with Motown. His friends gathered around us in a loose half circle.

Motown's face was blank. He didn't rise to the bait Martize was dangling in his face. I didn't particularly like this ritual of male possession and dominance but I knew first hand Motown never fought over a female. For one, if need be, but never over one. He said there were too many women in the world for such nonsense.

I was glad he thought that way for everyone's sake. He was out sized by all three chipmunks with Martize and even Martize himself, though shorter, was heavier.

"Sup?" Martize shot at him.

"What you want to be up?" he replied calmly enough.

Inwardly I groaned. Last time I heard him say that he'd wound up breaking the dude's arm and nose. Did he honestly think he could take them all? Carmen would fight with him but I doubted even her skills would be enough to turn the tide. These guys were that big.

"We're running Martize," I said as the knife to their tension. "Let's go somewhere quiet ok?"

"Why don't we let them talk." Carmen took my lead. "We'll be at Hooters if you need us, Meghan."

She grandly took Motown's hand and placed it on her ass after she curled up into him like a ballroom dancer. I knew it was just a show but when he fell into the roll naturally by kissing her neck then popping her ass hard enough that we heard it over the crowd and games and she purred as if she enjoyed it—which she probably did!—well I found myself just a little jealous. Croft's panties I didn't know why.

We watched them flirt their way across to Hooters before I eyed Martize.

"What're you doing here?" Carmen and Motown had planted a seed of suspicion.

However I was adamantly trying to be a loyal girlfriend.

We've been dating for little more than 12 months; have been exclusive for the last six. We met at Starbucks where he'd paid for my drink and said with a disarming smile, "You didn't expect to go Dutch on our first date did you?" I'd immediately labeled him a drug dealer due to his baggy jeans, KG Timberwolves jersey topped with music video jewels and a wad of cash in a rubber band but his approach was so unique I couldn't hide a smile.

Upon further research, a few dates, I learned he wasn't a drug dealer just a good barber and poker player. Eventually I introduced him to Eric who hired him as a barber which led to him becoming a part-time fixture at Naq.

"I'm trying to figure out why my girl is dressed like a video vixen hugged up with another nigga." He waved in Motown's general direction.

His dark eyes were pinched in anger I didn't quite deserve. We weren't technically "hugged up" but he probably wouldn't care about semantics at the moment. As a square jawed brawny man Martize had confidence to last a lifetime; seeing him jealous and protective was new to me.

"A video vixen?" I challenged sharply.

A dressing room mirror had shown me a Meghan in blue, white, gray, and pink patterned pants that flowed down my hips becomingly before tapering into my boots. The blouse was way risqué and a little over the top in my mind but it was no less sexy for being so. White and sheer everywhere except my boobs it tucked into my pants and would've shown much more skin if not for the royal blue vest that didn't button and matched my new lacy lingerie.

"Are you trying to march in here with Alvin, Simon, and Theodore," I waved my French tipped hand at the trio of mutated chipmunks, "and call me a ho?"

"Ain't no one calling you a ho," He soothed. "I just let my temper get the best of me, but imagine how I must feel when I'm on the way to buy my girl a birthday present then have a few drinks with some homies when I get a call saying my girl is more than a little cozy with another nigga.

"Imagine," he continued reasonably, holding onto my shoulders, eyes earnest, "how I must feel when I try to call but her phone goes straight to voicemail then I find her playing video games with said guy."

He pulled me into a hug.

"I imagine it might be upsetting," I conceded into his chest.

"Plus I was a little dazzled to see you dressed so...provocatively," he whispered in my ear.

I was not letting him off that easy. "That's all good and dandy as Lara Croft panties but who are these chipmunks who know me by sight when I don't even recognize them?"

This entire time they'd stood there without a word, close enough to hear but far enough to seem unobtrusive. I didn't particularly like them. They were acting too much like sentinels.

"They're just drinking buddies," he said dismissively. "Now can I steal you away for a few moments?"

He gave me his version of the look.

"There's no time for that, I have a run to finish."

He kissed me lightly. "Aight, just hit me up when you're done."

He left with his chipmunks but left me feeling worried.

XX

"Every guy who sees me tonight, I'm gonna be the envy of," Motown sang as he eyed Carmen and I with open appreciation. "With the baddest by my side, when I walk up in the club. Ohhh..."

We smiled as he snapped pictures on his LG Envy as we posed before a water fountain in the Mall. Carmen looked resplendent in a white-wine colored dress with a modestly cut out diamond on the back but a plunging neckline that went low enough to display her toned pierced belly. Her shoes were an open toed sparkly affair with sky high stilettos.

We both wore chandelier earrings and a rose-gold rose pendent Motown pinned on our dress.

If I had to guess I would've said he wanted us coordinated because while I had on my pearlescent dress he was looking ultra GQ in a cream suit with a glossy ivory shirt and Italian loafers. In his left ear was a small masculine hoop earring with diamonds encrusting the center all the way around.

Nothing either of us wore except our underwear, maybe, cost less than 200 dollars and I couldn't begin to care about all the fancy names. But the beauty of it all, the feel of it against my skin made me appreciate why people loved expensive cloths. Even the panties felt like a cloud against my nana.

Still the stares we garnered as we made our way back to the lockers we'd been using for storage were a little unnerving.

I was used to people ogling my ass but this was different. This made me self-conscious.

These two, however, were basking in it, strutting as though they were superstars. I appreciated how beautiful we all looked but their swaggering confidence made me feel pale in comparison.

Motown gave us each a prepaid Visa "just in case" as we filled our clutches with the important things that would fit. Carmen stuck the Visa down her dress while giving me a you-never-know shrug when I cocked a quizzical brow at her. Still I followed suit.

"At least I know two places my credit is welcome," Motown quipped, grinning rakishly.

"Don't you mean four?" Carmen flirted.

"Touché."

I began to wonder if there was really chemistry between them when my train of thought was derailed by two suspicious men. Both wore black suits with white shirts and black ties. One was tall, the other barely 5 feet, both were compact, self-possessed, and black and white respectively.

Black looked around carefully after studying the screen of his cell phone. Seeing us he tapped his partner then nodded in our direction.

"Motown," I turned slightly to him, "there're two guys in suits and shades heading our way."

He wasn't worried in the least. "I know, I saw them when they came in."

They stopped a few feet away from us.

"Mr. Motown," Black said. "I'm Dre and this is Patrick. We've been instructed to assist you if you need it tonight. Tony will be your chauffer for the night."

"Chauffer?" I blurted as Motown nodded and handed over our keys. "How'd you...when'd you...?"

He grinned as if he knew what I meant while shaking his hands as if they were hot.

"These hands are certifiably blessed, all they do is collect connects."

"All I know, Bubblegum panties," Carmen whispered in my ear, "is that you better put a claim on him before you and your nana miss the chance of a lifetime because someone steals him away."

I watched as she gave her bags to Patrick and sashayed towards our waiting limo but couldn't decide if that was a warning, threat, or promise.

CH7

By the time we were safely ensconced in the black stretch Hummer it had been snowing longer than a Halo party on Red Bulls and seemed just as unlikely to be near abating anytime soon. With six inches of steadily rising snow I didn't begrudge our driver his duty.

Any other time we would've enjoyed the overwhelming luxury of the limo but as it was the bottle of chilled VSOP went untouched, none of the numerous TVs were on, and the dark leather seats trimmed in gold held no visual appeal. Even the speakers were silent.

We all sat facing the raised partition, lost in our own silence. Carmen was on Motown's left while I occupied the space to his right. Her head was back, eyes closed, although she wasn't asleep. Motown was repeatedly flexing his hands. Nervous tension filled the air.

"Meghan," he suddenly turned to me, "can I rub your legs?" Clearly a plea.

He's more nervous than he let on I realized. Then a thought stuck me, *we all deal with fucked up situations in different ways*. Was physical contact his way of coping? Insight struck and a lot of things about Motown made sense in a new way. His subtle way of blending tactile responses into his conversations. His ability to get just about any female to cuddle. Why every girl I'd ever seen him with was so touchy feely towards him.

I understood him a lot more in that moment.

Now we were heading into a situation we could scarcely control without knowing any more about the man who wanted to meet than the sound of his voice. And save for the pen knives, little six inch blades disguised as ink pens, Tony had given us courtesy of his boss we were weaponless.

His anxiety was understandable.

Being careful not to flash him I gave him my feet. He held them up in one hand then deftly removed my heels before setting them in his lap. It had been pointless trying to keep him from seeing up my dress; he hadn't even tried to look.

I silently scoffed at myself: he'd already seen me naked.

He sighed as his hands began to glide across my legs. He almost made me sigh with him. His first few passes from the ball of my foot to the back of my knee were exploratory, searching for knots and tension I hadn't even realized were there until he plucked at them like a serenading Spanish guitarist. My eyes drooped in pleasure.

He leaned his head back to stare at the sunroof and said, "So here's what we know. Before Meghan took this run someone warned her off. Then, someone, possibly the same someone or ones, violently tried to stop her. She has yet to be attacked since the hotel"

"Does that mean we rid ourselves of that nuisance or are they being more cautious?" Carmen asked.

"I'd lean towards cautious but there's no way to tell. Meanwhile," he continued, "there's Mystery man, who I suspect might be the owner of this club. I can't figure out why he called us here and that bothers me but Eric verified him in his own way so the package is definitely his."

"Maybe he wants verification we still have it," I ventured, suppressing a groan as he turned my legs into liquid fire. If I felt like this after only a minute or two when his mind was only half focused on his task what must his clients feel when he's fully focused?

I shivered at the thought.

His hands stilled. "You alright?"

Snapping my finger into a thumbs up I smiled. "Oooh joy."

"That could be it," he allowed with a knowing smile, "or it could be something else entirely. What we do know is Club Sin is a three story refurbished warehouse with plenty of floor space and four exits."

"You're expecting trouble," Carmen said pointedly.

Motown scoffed and grinned wanly. "You know why I am a better soldier than I was a drug dealer?"

"Alicia says you lacked the knack for it," I answered honestly.

He shook his head in obvious disappointment. "All these years and she still doesn't get it. Alicia is a hustler's wife so the streets thrill her and she'll never understand anyone who it doesn't thrill. It's not that I lacked a knack for it, I can sell silk to a silkworm, it's that I lacked the taste for it."

He paused as he gazed off to some place we couldn't begin to see. His hands slowed with the memory. His voice was soft yet wry when he continued. "I've always had this sixth sense about people that's layered with suspicion and makes me wary of everybody." He smiled ruefully. "There were times E thought I had something to do with a life threatening situation after I'd proven my suspicions."

"Now he trusts you implicitly," I said, remembering his declaration.

Motown never let me down.

"I've done two tours in Iraq and have saved a lot of lives because of my natural suspicions..." he shook his head, falling silent again, lost in his thoughts.

After a few minutes Carmen impatiently asked, "So what's your point?"

Sighing he patted her thigh. "My point is, everybody is suspect so I always expect trouble."

XX

We spotted the club half a mile away.

Located on a back road well clear of residential neighborhoods it would've been impossible to miss. It was lit up brighter than Time Square's New Year's Eve ball and even had a bat signal with the word Sinful replacing the bat. It flashed randomly, drawing the eye like a libidinous strike of lightning.

Floor plans might've said it was a warehouse but an architect would debate that. Vociferously. It had a dome with naughty suggestive gargoyles contrasting against the black sky. What caught my eye was the glassed in awning that wrapped around the building. Lights within the glass changed colors as we circled the building, going from color to color without any logical order. As we watched one section faded from neon blue to the darkness of black lights so that only bright colors worn by waiting patrons were seen like ghostly figures.

"Quite a few white dresses in that group," Motown mused wryly.

"Leave it to you to latch onto panties and bras," Carmen scoffed.

He laughed as he gave his signature unapologetic shrug. "I am what I am."

"Perverted?" I teased.

"Egotistical?" Carmen added.

"Keep on," he grinned, "and I'm gonna bend both of ya'll over my knee and give you one egotistically perverted spanking!"

"Promises promises," Carmen tsked at his threatening hand.

Tony came over the speaker to let us know we were at the VIP entrance and asked if we were ready.

We all soberly looked at one another and nodded in turn. Motown lowered the partition and told him we were as ready as we'd ever be. Tony walked around and opened our door. Motown stepped out before holding out a hand for us to follow.

I shivered automatically as freezing wind bit into my exposed skin. It snuck in under my hem and began a war with the warmth within. After taking a few steps we were met by a wall of heat that reminded me of a blow dryer. Another foot and I realized there must've been a hidden heating system.

Inside the awning it was warmer than a mild summer day. Off to our right was the line which nearly circled the building. We were separated by a booth from those who apparently weren't VIP. Ahead of us was a small group of five women whose skin tones reminded me of flavors of Betty Crocker's cake mixes.

One was arguing with the big bald bouncer. His body language, folded arms over a thick chest and weary scowl, said he'd had just about enough of her.

"The website says if you arrive in a limo you get into VIP," she argued. "My invite-"

"Neither excuses or exempts you from the dress code or the limit of guests your invite allows. These rules are not suggestions and are therefore not open to interpretation."Motown and Carmen shared a look I couldn't quite decipher before he shrugged and said;

"I'm sure you can handle this."

"Meghan," she turned to me, "let me see your invite."

Without a second thought I pulled up the invite then gave her my phone. She read it, nodded, then tapped the closest girl on her shoulder and asked the protagonista's name.

"Autumn but-"

"Don't worry," Carmen interrupted, "I got you."

She excused herself through the small throng until she made Autumn's side. Autumn had a red velvet complexion, short brown hair, a slim frame, and was only as tall as Carmen's boobs.

"Autumn let me lend you a hand," Carmen offered.

Autumn looked taken aback. "Who are you?"

"I'm the best thing that's happened to you all night." Then she leaned down and whispered in her ear. I would've given up next year's tickets to Country Fest to hear what she told her. One moment Autumn was tense, brown eyes inflamed with anger, and the next she was nodding thoughtfully. Finally she began blushing so hard you would've thought someone splashed paint on her cheeks.

She nodded at something Carmen whispered before Carmen reached into her purse and turned her back on us. Motown pulled the last four into a reluctant huddle, quietly capturing their attention while Carmen addressed the bouncer. She leaned in close, his eyes darted down, whether to her awesome cleavage or the money she'd no doubt proffered him I couldn't tell, and drew a nod from him too. She showed our invite, he nodded again, then turned back to us as she handed back my phone with a satisfied smile.

"Well that's settled," she said. "Ladies, I'm gonna take Autumn out to my limo to see if we can't do something about her attire while ya'll wait for us inside." She took Autumn's handand led her out.

"Ya'll coming in or what?" Motown asked playfully.

"We don't even know your name," The fudge chocolate one of the group said with an African accent.

He took her answer as a yes, wrapped his arms around two girls' shoulders, and told them, "All in due time. For now tell me what ya'll are drinking."

They faded into the club and I followed.

I'm not into clubs like Alicia, Carmen, and, apparently, Motown are. Usually I'll go if they call but the idea of bumping and grinding with strange men has obviously lost its appeal. Still, with that being said, I couldn't believe my eyes once we were inside.

Suspended from the ceiling at varying levels were dancers in clear bubbles. A few were men, most were women but all were sleek and athletic dressed in some mesh fabric and skimpy lacy underwear with a white mask that depicted faces in the throes of passion.

A hostess materialized out of the darkness in a crimson mini skirt shaped like an S. Not until a beam of light played over her did I realize the entire "dress" wasn't a dress at all but paint so skillfully applied I could hardly tell the difference.

Club Sin indeed! I thought as she asked for our invite. She looked it over, smiled, then asked us to follow her. We followed.

Motown had the group of girls giggling at something he was saying by then. He caught my eye over one girl's platinum blond shoulder to offer up a bored roll of his chocolate eyes.

Why are you entertaining them? my eyes questioned.

We were led up an ascending ramp-like walkway along one wall to our own richly appointed private room. There a beige leather square shaped couch, broken only by the doors, fit to the walls of the room and a black table in the middle of the room. The last wall was made entirely of glass with a slider door which opened onto the dance floor. Large flat screen TVs posted over both couches displayed a rotating view of dancers all over the club.

Whatever I expected I didn't get it. This was luxurious, sensual, decadent even.

"Here's the controls for the sound," the hostess showed us a touch screen panel on the wall, "the cameras for the TVs which can be changed like so, and the call button for your waitress if you need anything. Her name is Belisandre...well here she is now."

"Hellooo," Belisandre greeted cheerfully.

She was every bit as painted as her peer except she had a... bouncier figure and symmetrical features. In the dimly lit room her canted blue eyes were brighter than a Siberian Husky's.

She carried a bottle of Rosé with sparklers arrayed around it. The party girls squealed.

"My name's Belisandre," her voice was soft and slightly lilted. "I'll be taking care of you this evening."

Motown stepped up to her, deftly sliding a 50 onto her tray and quietly ordering two bottles of Sprite or any non-alcoholic beverage in a bottle. She nodded and left us to our own devices.

"Well, lovelies," he said while hoisting the bottle, "let the real fun begin!"

Miss fudge turned up the music, some Chris Brown mix, and they all began dancing as Motown freely poured the liquor.

I turned away, looking out over the dance floor. Motown's reflection approached me from behind. He took both of my hands and placed them on the glass as he whispered Spanish in my ear.

"Just relax, Meghan, dance a little so we can talk."

Only his comment made me notice how tense I'd suddenly become. Taking a deep breath I closed the distance he'd left between us and rocked slowly, heedless of the pumping music around us. He suddenly chuckled deep in his chest. I froze and our eyes met in the window.

"What's so funny?"

"I just spotted Carmen and Autumn and thought of the theme song to a show I watched as a shorty: where in the world is Carmen San Diego?"

He sang the ditty and I bit my lip. I've admitted he can sing. I've admitted that even a dead nun would be hard put to ignore his singing voice. Even half singing a ditty he had a tonal quality that's just... sexy. With him pressed against me, whispering fluently in Spanish, and singing...well boyfriend or no I could no longer deny that he could turn me on. Did turn me on.

I hid it deep though. Underestimating him was becoming problematic. He was smoother than I'd given him credit for. He could probably seduce all those little floozies and they'd all die of bliss for the pleasure of his company.

He didn't need a damaged girl like me when he could have damn near any woman he wanted.

I focused on trying to spot Carmen in the vastness that was the dance floor but instead found my gaze drawn to blinking lights in another booth. A man in the doorway toasted me with a raised glass. The gesture was unmistakably meant for me.

"Guess he would put us in a booth so he'd know where we are," Motown said wryly as if he'd missed the obvious.

So he wasn't infallible. Did I trust him any less? No. I had stopped dancing but he hadn't stopped holding me. His scent surrounded me; some subtly spicy cologne blending perfectly with the lavender baby oil and powder I knew he wore every day.

I pressed my forehead against the glass door. Two years I had ignored his advances and here I was in a day, tortured by his closeness.

"Why are you still here?" I whispered, hoping that he wouldn't hear me, fearing the answering when he did.

"It's where I-"

Belisandre returned laden with a sizzling tray of steak and chicken. Motown let me turn around without another word. There was grilled pineapple, limes, kiwi, and a strawberry topped cheesecake along with four bottles of Fiji water that a second waitress carried in behind Belisandre.

The party girls squealed.

Belisandre smiled at Motown, showing sparkling even teeth that were as bright as her eyes. She handed him a note, her fingers gliding along his unnecessarily.

"Fiji water is the best I could do."

He grabbed two bottles, checked the note, then handed it and a bottle to me. He thanked her as one of the party girls drew his attention.

I tuned them out and read the card.

You know where I am. Please join me when you're ready.

Whatever the name was I couldn't read it because it was scrawled like a million doctors' signatures.

"Another bottle for the ladies," Motown cheered.

Squeal.

He slid Belisandre another 50 and her blue eyes beamed with a smile. It was a smile that brought Carmen's warning to mind but I wondered how another female could steal what didn't belong to me.

I spun and left the room in a rush.

Motown caught up with me before I'd taken 10 purposeful strides. We threaded our way through the crowded dance floor. I spotted Carmen being grinded on by Autumn. She was close and gave me the I'm watching you fingers. I nodded understanding.

Mystery man opened the door for us himself. I expected someone tall and domineering but he barely topped 5'2". He was compact with an angular face, milk chocolate skin and dark eyes that were all the darker thanks to his charcoal suit.

There was a fountain of white chocolate flowing on his table. Around the base was an assortment of fruit and chocolate bars. There were also two women occupying a couch... and themselves. One had straight black hair that draped down her legs as she sat. I swear she looked like a life sized Jasmine from Aladdin. Her friend had golden brown skin and honey brown hair that twisted and curled upon itself. Her full breast hung free from her dress as if she didn't have a care in the world.

Jasmine reached over to grab a chocolate bar, broke a finger length piece, drizzled it in chocolate then stuck it between her teeth and fed it to Honey while squeezing her boobs.

"At least someone's properly entertained," I murmured.

Motown and I separated to different sides of the room as Mystery man calmly walked over to the women and said something in a language I couldn't understand. They both left after serving us a small plate of mixed fruit and chocolate drizzled with white chocolate.

He turned down his reggae music before sitting so leisurely one might think he had not a care in the world. The screen above his head showed a steaming pool and bar with a male and female bartender. The pool was full of half-naked and completely nude bodies. I trained my eyes onto his, thankful that there wasn't any sound.

"I hope you have enjoyed my hospitality," he finally said. His voice was every bit as dark and sinister as before.

"You have interesting ideas, Mr. Domeer," Motown answered.

His answer reminded me that while JT hadn't been able to find a photo of the club's owner he had found his name. Motown had found it suspicious that a business owner didn't even have a DMV photo and suspected he might be our benefactor. I hadn't thought any of that so kudos to him.

"Yes," Domeer acknowledged, "but we must remember we have but one life to live so I live mine to the fullest." He leaned forward, snapped off a piece of Cookies-n-Cream, then sat back to savor it.

I nibbled on a piece of my own Cookies-n-Cream.

"That's all good and dandy like Lara Croft panties but I'm a little concerned you called us here."

"As you should be," he agreed, regarding me with eyes as dark as spilled oil. "Someone found out I contracted your services and subsequently attempted to intervene. I did not appreciate their interference.

"Fortunately, having never used your services before I was forced to acknowledge only someone close to me with firsthand knowledge could have known my intentions." He paused for more chocolate.

"Is it safe to say you figured out who this unfortunate soul is?" I asked before biting into a succulent strawberry.

"I have been informed that certain individuals had paraded around as uniformed cops and that the real cops were having difficulties finding the culprit."

He gave us a meaningful look. Neither of us reacted. He nodded as if he'd expected no less.

"I have been informed there are no longer questions about those unfortunate circumstances."

"He or she was obviously not working alone, were you informed as to whom they were working with?" Motown asked.

"There was a list provided. However, all but three names on it are accounted for; Chopper, Thunder, and Tease."

My eyes shot to Motown. I swallowed, feeling a slight buzzing begin in my head.

"Do those names mean something to you?"

"Croft's panties I hope not," I sighed while running a hand slowly down my face.

"We'll have to check into it," Motown hedged.

Domeer shrugged. "It is only a concern of mine if it prevents you from making your delivery."

Hadn't Motown said there were very few chances of happenstances? Could I just ignore so blatant a red flag? Even if I could Motown wouldn't. Carmen definitely wouldn't. Domeer didn't look like the type to flinch at torturing someone for an answer but he seemed sure the names hadn't been slurred by an abused mouth.

Tease. I closed my eyes against the rush of emotions.

Martize. Tease. Tease .Martize.

Why? I cried silently. Why would Martizę have anything to do with this? What would he have to gain? Why would he want to hurt me?

"What," I asked, feeling a flush of anger heating my skin, "is so damn important about your package that people are ready to kill me over it?"

We weren't supposed to ask questions but I suddenly didn't care.

"What you're carrying is a fourth of a bigger object and in itself is worth a few million to the right person. Imagine what the whole is worth."

I stood and nodded, suddenly restless... full of energy... invigorated as if I had live wires instead of veins. I started pacing from where I stood to where Motown sat and back again.

"Greed can be a powerful motivator," Motown said.

"Indeed," Domeer agreed. "Unfortunately that is only part of my problem, one you need not worry yourselves with."

I stopped suddenly as a shudder ran through me. It began in my belly and spread throughout my body. I could literally feel it tingle my scalp and toes.

I knew this feeling like I knew no other.

My eyes took in the half eaten plate of goodies then the fountain. Heat suffused my skin.

I drained the entire bottle of water. My chest heaved. My nana was on fire.

Motown eyed me warily.

I locked eyes with Domeer but his gaze gave away nothing. Motown, I noticed, hadn't touched his plate. Domeer hadn't actually eaten from the fountain unlike the tongue swapping beauties who'd given us our plates.

Covered in white chocolate.

Drugged white chocolate.

I know what it's like to be doped up, God knows I do, and I don't particularly like it. That's why I don't smoke weed or drink. I don't even like taking Advil for a headache.

Now here I stand with something coursing through my system that had my libido spiking harder than retail stocks on black Friday.

"Meghan?" Motown stood in front of me so close I could count his thick eyelashes. I hadn't even seen him move.

I couldn't say this aloud, though. There was no way Domeer didn't know there was some kind of stimulant in the fountain. I refused to give him the satisfaction of knowing how it was affecting me. I couldn't even fully blame him because he hadn't forced me to eat it. Instead I drew in a deep breath. I could control this. But oh joy if my dress didn't feel a little smoother against my skin.

I took Motown's bottle and gulped it down.

"I'm fine," I lied. "I just need some air."

I trusted him to step in so I grabbed my clutch and left him to it. The glass door was warm against my back and I didn't even care if they were watching me as I leaned there.

Bass heavy rap pounded into my bones as an angel in a bubble with pure rapture on her face slowly floated by. What would an angel know of rapture? Could one even have sex in Heaven? I've seen paintings of devils and people in Hell having orgies but not once have I seen an angel getting laid.

A girly giggle bubbled up from nowhere at the thought.

I moved from Domeer's booth giggling so hard tears came to my eyes. The thought tickled me so much my stomach hurt. I giggled my way to a bar, thankful I couldn't see the bartender's face behind his mask.

I ordered water and headed towards a rear exit so that I could get some fresh country air.

I knew without a doubt that's what I needed; water and fresh air.

I found an exit and wound up in the glass awning. Thankfully no one was around. I stepped to another door, thinking I'd go far enough to get a blast of fresh cold air.

What I got was an arm around my throat, a sharp prick in my neck, then sudden darkness.

CH8

Panic nearly overwhelmed me.

When I first came to fear was the first thing I felt. It soured my mouth and cramped my belly. My heart felt like hummingbird wings in my chest. Nausea followed Fear like a float in a parade.

I puked.

It must not have been my first time because I heard a worried voice ask if someone was sure I was unconscious. The reply was broken up as I heaved up bile but it came down to that guy saying it must be a reaction to the drug they'd given me. According to him I'd be out a least another two hours and by then we'd be...another heave and I missed out again.

I slid across metal and couldn't hide a grunt as my back banged into a wall. Cracking my eyes I found myself on the back floor of a cargo van. They must've trusted their drug to keep me subdued because I wasn't secured at all.

If they didn't care about me escaping they certainly didn't care about me getting hurt either. I slid towards the front seats as the driver came to a snow crunching stop. A stoplight's red glow basked the interior enough that I made out the bald pates of two of the chipmunks.

My heart sank even as it broke.

Martize was definitely caught up in this somehow. That irritated me. I had trusted him, been duped, and now he was betraying me for money? How could I have been such a dumbass? How could I have been so blind?

I slid against the back door like so much dirty laundry. My body was weak, weaker than after a 5k marathon but I'd take that.

Slightly stronger was stronger than they'd expected to leave me.

Snow blurred the windshield as if angry I'd been snatched. Hopefully it'd slow them down enough that I could recover. A turn had me sliding again. I caught a glimpse of my clutch on the floor between their seats. If I could fight off this weakness I might be able to get it. I silently thanked Domeer for feeding me his stimulant.

Motown didn't believe in happenstances. I understood the irony.

Putting what energy I could muster into each wiggle I slowly managed to inch my way toward my purse. My heel was inches away when the van began another turn which threatened to slide me away.

I lunged. Missed.

I could've cried as I slid around.

"Dog, she's like a rag doll back there," Passenger joked.

Driver grunted, his attention on the road.

Shutting my eyes I took a deep breath before I collided with another wall. I needed it to appear like I was still unconscious, true, but more than that the effort had exhausted me. Plus my dress was bunched up around my waist and Passenger was talking about my nana.

I had enough on my plate without the threat of another panic attack. That would make everything worse. Some memories, however, don't fade with time.

Images of Derrick and Ira flashed through my mind. Derrick habitually flashing his top teeth like a braying donkey as he called himself the Panty Snatcher. Ira forcing me to run on a treadmill then stealing away my sweaty panties. The images flew by. Ira. Derrick. Derrick. Ira.

I can count the ways that I hate them.

Using that hatred I cracked my eyes, counted the ways, and inched back towards my purse. I focused on those feeling instead of letting them swamp me like a rogue wave. Anger. Despair. Loneliness. Indignation. Shame. Every emotion I'd ever felt towards two bitch ass cousins who couldn't take no for an answer gave me strength.

Inches away we slowly came to a stop.

I slid forward, heels poking my clutch.

"Just look at that round ass and tell me you don't want none," Passenger wheedled.

"I can wait and you can too," Driver said with finality.

"Dog, you're crazy."

I just knew I'd be caught when I slid and my purse slid backwards with me. We turned and I lost track of it for a moment. It stopped behind me but I'd have to turn over to reach it.

Driver suddenly swore. The van bounced off of something that made us go into a spin. I flipped over and my boob landed on the clutch as Carrie Underwood's Jesus take the wheel sprang into my head.

I pulled my dress down as much as I dared as we came to a stop but it barely covered my ass. When we came to a stop I was laying perpendicular to both seats, face down on my belly.

"What the hell did you hit?"

"How should I know I can't see shit in this blizzard."

"Well, go check for damage."

There was ruffling then cold air streamed through Driver's open door before it whoomped closed. Passenger clicked on the overhead light. He grunted "Hmm hmm hmm," a second before I felt his hand on my ass.

"Don't know why Teaser waited so long but I don't give a damn what Chopper says. I been waiting a long time to get a taste of you and I'll be damned if I wait another second."

While he spoke he kept squeezing my ass and running his fingers around the edge of my panties. It took everything in me to keep playing possum.

"Royal blue, silk laced princess cut thong," his voice had a dreamy quality to it. "At least you have good taste. You'll never know this but I was the one who taught Derrick and Ira the joy of a woman's panties: she leaves a part of herself in every pair."

He made a sound of disgust as he squeezed my nana painfully and I was so glad he couldn't see my face. There was no way he would've missed my grimace.

"Then you had the nerve to kill Derrick and now Teaser wants to live up to his name."

I could've kissed Chopper when his door opened and Passengers hand darted away.

"What is it?" he snarled.

"Flat tire, I'll need your help."

He grumbled then they left me alone.

How I wanted to cry! I didn't understand what was going on but more than that I felt shocked stupid. Was Martize somehow related to Ira and Derrick?

Had I been tricked and seduced for some kind of sick revenge?

I rolled onto my back and, not even daring to pull my dress back down for fear of alerting them, shook my limbs out. I dashed away the tears clouding my eyes as I searched for my phone.

It wasn't there and save for an ink pen and a tampon it was empty.

I sat up to see if they'd left anything useful and spotted a black Motorola when I heard the rear doors jangle. I slumped back down onto my purse not even a second before the double doors opened.

Snow gusted in.

They didn't notice my shiver as they pulled out the necessary gear. The doors whoomped closed.

I shot up as fast as I could and snatched up the phone. My heart sank twice. For one it was prepaid so even if I managed 911 there was no way they could trace the call even if I managed to leave the line open. All of which was moot.

There was no signal.

Putting the phone back I looked around for anything I might use as a weapon. Found nothing. I almost threw my purse away in frustration when I remembered.

There was an ink pen in it. Motown's six inch ceramic knife.

I choked out a tearful, thankful, laugh. Eric had told me at the beginning of this run that Motown never let him down.

On my own now I don't know what that meant for me but I wasn't exactly helpless and now would be the time to help myself. With a twist he'd demonstrated earlier I popped the top off the double edged stiletto then transferred the top to the bottom for a grip.

I lay back down as the rear doors jangled open.

On the inside I was smiling,

They thought I was weak. They thought I was helpless. They thought I was at their mercy.

They thought wrong.

I remember the first few weeks into my captivity how I had blamed my papa for getting me into that mess. Logically I knew he'd been dead three years and had nothing whatsoever to do with it but in a situation like that it's not always about logic. Still I blamed him because I'd felt invincible enough to get caught slipping.

Papa had been as wide as three men, more solid than marble pillars, and possessed a joyful strength Mama adored. I was born stout and Papa loved that I wasn't fragile. He taught me everything he considered practical that school wouldn't; from hunting with rifles, bow, and traps, to fishing, camping, wrestling and kickboxing.

Mama would have a fit when I came in bruised up from a fight but Papa would just ask me who won and laugh as he hugged me. I'll be the first to admit I grew into just another teen who thought she had it all figured out. I was confident in my strength and my skills. Too confident as it turned out because I was able to be drugged and kidnapped.

Yea, well, I survived that and if I have any say in the matter I'll survive this too I told myself as the duo opened the rear doors. They tossed their Jack and tire iron in a hurry before hustling back into their respective seats. Passenger sparked up a Black and Mild.

"Dog, check your phone now that the storm's clearing."

"We gotta find a landline; I never get a signal out here."

I slid to the back door as we accelerated, bumping my shoulder on the unsecured Jack. I added that to my list of insults as I prepped myself for the struggle ahead.

I waited until we were well under way and I felt a lot stronger than I had when I first came to. My heart raced nervously but I felt good otherwise. Good enough to slide my way towards the front seats. Good enough to rise to my knees so neither saw me.

Good enough to jab my knife right into Chopper's corded neck. He choked as the blade parted skin and muscle like a hot knife through snow.

"Fuck?" Passenger looked up wild eyed as I jerked the knife forward.

Blood sprayed all over the steering wheel and dash. Passenger grabbed the wheel instinctively when Chopper grasped at his throat in vain. I reversed the blade with a practiced flick of my thumb before stabbing at Passenger. He partially blocked it but my momentum drove the point into his eye.

He screamed, jerked away and took the wheel with him.

The van hit a snow bank and all I had time to do was ball up as we went airborne. The van flipped two or three times before my head and the Jack collided somewhere in midair.

I couldn't count any more flips after that.

CH9

Dealing with the aftermath of killing is much harder than the kill.

In my world at least.

Some people can cope with taking a life, some even enjoy it, but I'm not such a bad ass.

I could blame my dry heaves on a probable concussion or I could blame it on the garish sight of Chopper hanging upside down in his seatbelt with the front of his neck gaping like a lightless tunnel to his tainted soul.

The coppery tang of blood mixed with the pungent reek of Black and Mild as I shakily wiped blood off my face, knowing I couldn't have been out long. The van was still running, the cigar still burning, my head still throbbed and the blood from the tender gash on my head still flowed.

It hurt to move my left arm. A huge bruise from forearm to bicep made me wince.

Dizziness took me for a ride so I sat for a while.

I felt horrible but I knew I couldn't stay here. Passenger groaned and rolled over onto his stomach. He looked around with his one good eye, hand over the other, and found me sitting with my back against the rear doors. He sat up and glared at me hatefully.

My knife clattered to the roof from his coat.

"You bitch. You ornery, good for nothing bitch." He picked up the knife; it looked like a straw in his meaty grip.

He hobbled towards me on his knees, blood weeping from his eye.

"You killed my nephews. Now you've gone and murdered my brother. You tried to kill me but now I gotchu all to myself." His head nearly reached what should've been the ceiling but he weaved drunkenly.

I waited...until he was just inside my kicking range to pull my legs up and flash my panties. As I'd hoped the perv couldn't resist a look.

I lashed out at his left knee. Connected with a brick-like thigh and for a moment feared that I'd underestimated him. But he snarled and toppled sideways as his leg slid from beneath him. I followed up with a side-ish kick towards his face.

He cried out as his head jerked back but somehow managed to catch my next kick. My heel slid off in his hand and I wasted no time lashing out lower. It thumped into his ribs. He threw my heel at me then lunged as I blocked it.

My right hand fell on the tire iron but it didn't register at first. I brought both feet up to stop his lunge but even with both planted on his massive chest I barely slowed him down.

My knees pressed hard into my chest. He caught me with a heavy right cross that rocked me and made me curl into an even tighter ball.

His eye gleamed in triumph.

But he didn't know me well enough. I'm a kick boxer. My legs are my strongest muscle and he only had me pinned under a fraction of his weight. His punch hurt but it pissed me off more despite the ringing in my head.

Screaming, I pushed with all my might, ignoring the dizziness that threatened to whoop my ass.

He flew and hit the "ceiling" then landed awkwardly on the Jack. I hustled up to my knees with the tire iron and, screaming curses, wasted no time at all smashing his knees. I had room to put every ounce of anger into my swings but even through his snow pants they cracked.

You taught Derrick and Ira. Whack. They raped me. Whack. Humiliated me. Whack. You wanted revenge for their deaths. Whack. You groped me without my permission. Whack. You wanted to revisit all the horrors I had escaped. Whack. You wanted to steal my panties. whack.

"You wanted to steal my CHOICE!"

By then he lay in a blubbering heap broken by what a coroner would call blunt force trauma. It was easy to jab the crowbar's slender point into his face. He jerked away in a final attempt to escape and it tore its way deep into his ear. He spasmed. Once. Twice.

I fell away, dry heaving from the sight. Why did people keep forcing me to kill them? He wanted revenge for a problem he'd created. How could he be mad at me for escaping? They had been wrong! It wasn't my fault. I hadn't asked to be their victim.

I closed my heart like valves on a dam and set my mind on the task of disrobing them. They both wore cold weather gear and as much as I loathed the thought I knew if I was going to make it even half a mile away from this death trap I'd have to wear more than my dress and heels.

They were layered against the cold; furred parkas, furred leather insulated gloves, formfitting snow pants, a turtle neck sweater, a one-piece long john-ish suit that fit them like Under Armor apparel, thick socks and waterproof boots.

Passenger was taller and wider but I managed to fill out the important parts of the long john suit thanks to my curves. It was a little long at the wrist and ankles but was semi-smooth and warm so I kept my mind practical.

With the adrenaline wearing off I had to brace myself against a seat to curb a dizzy spell.

I wondered how far I could go if I had a concussion.

As far as you have to I told myself.

I kept my dress on. It would only help with the layers and filling in empty space inside these cloths. I tucked the extra fabric into the socks but the boots were several sizes too big. Resting for a few minutes I tried not to nod off and succeeded.

What little light there was faded momentarily, leaving me in total darkness. Patting around located the dome light and a flick illuminated the space. I gagged but moved on.

I cut Chopper out of his harness, made a pack from his cloths and checked his shoe size; two sizes smaller but still four sizes too big. I stuffed socks into the toes and made due. It couldn't be any worse than walking in snow shoes.

Their pockets revealed a miscellaneous treasure; a box of wine flavored Black and Mild's with four cigars, a butane lighter, two thick clips of bills no smaller than 20, Motown's debit card, a half-eaten roll of Mentos—I ate two to rid my mouth of this vile taste of bile—and another prepaid phone with no signal. The clock read 3:21 A.M.

Someone had taken the time to put a password on it. Someone would've thought I worked for a phone company when I held a few buttons and reset it. No GPS so I remained clueless about my location and only Martize's number was in the call log. Whatever.

If I was playing World of War craft I would've cast a healing spell, maybe leveled up and been happy as a newb after her first solo mission when the glove box popped open. A sheathed fixed blade hunting knife, a holstered 9mm Smith and Wesson (fully loaded chamber and all),two full clips, a flashlight, a paper bag full of Chewy granola and protein bars, a half full bottle of Sobe juice and a ski mask fell at my feet along with a few random papers.

I silently thanked the chipmunks for being so generous and well prepared.

Using the extra boot laces as straps I added all of that to my makeshift pack except the pistol, flashlight, and a granola bar. The former of which occupied a pocket on either side while the chocolate chip flavored granola bar went into my mouth bit by bit.

It settled and stayed down. Oh joy.

Flashing the flashlight through the windshield and front door windows I concluded we'd landed in a ditch because snow rose sharply on both sides while ahead it was unbroken as far as the light shone. The windshield was cracked but not broken. A few well-placed donkey kicks changed that quickly enough.

Gloves and ski mask followed by the hood went on immediately before I crawled out. A sharp twinge in my bladder made me groan and wish I was a boy. I settled that issues as close to the heat of the cab as possible.

Then a thought hit me. I emptied the glass bottle into the snow. Wearing a dead man's clothes was as personal as I wanted to get. I climbed up the van, located the gas line and set to work. It took a few minutes but eventually I had myself an impromptu lamp. A couple more minutes and I managed to scrape my way up the side of the ditch. Bereft of gas the van's engine sputtered and died.

I tried getting some kind of bearing but was forced to take the good with the bad. There was no more snow but it was cloudy and windy. We were on an empty road but whatever tracks we'd made before during our highway 20 ride were completely covered.

I sighed heavily. There wasn't a tree, corn stalk, house, light or anything else significant one might use as a landmark. I drank some of the Sobe juice thoughtfully, ignoring my aches and pains as best I could.

It's a shame I couldn't trust the way the van lay as an indicator of which direction not to go to avoid Martize. It had flipped too much and while it wasn't crushed like a midnight cigarette neither was it as pristine as its floor model days.

Being from Wisconsin I recognized a rural road when I saw one but I didn't relish breaking a trail through snow that was about knee deep. What it all told me was that they'd planned on taking me somewhere secluded.

Which meant I couldn't trust any house I might find.

Oh joy.

XX

I could feel the cold working through my coat and below it. My whole torso itched with the beginning chill as if it were glazed in Winter's frozen kitchen. There was nowhere to camp that wasn't exposed to the wind so I walked on, searching for the next storm drain.

Three hours later I walked right into the dawn of a new day.

"Hello Sunrise."

"Hello Meghan."

"Are you taking control of Wind now?"

"No one controls Wind," it laughed.

"I only ask because I've been trudging along for hours and every few feet I sink into the snow with a heavy phlunk. Inevitably no amount of layers or exertion can keep out Cold but with wind's help it's becoming harder and harder to ignore. I see a storm drain up ahead, finally, so can you ask Wind to cut me a little slack so I can start a small fire?"

"I'll ask but I make no promises."

Wind gusted in answer.

I slid down a bank into a ditch with a cemented drain deep enough to hide in during a tornado. Tamping down the snow the best I could I made a seat with the parka and placed my back against the metal grate.

I thought about my papa as I made a little fort wall to break the wind and started a fire with the "lamp" and what materials would work the best. I could practically see him sitting across from me, smiling in his proud quiet way. His gray eyes would be bright, a sharp contrast to his buzzed black hair. He'd say, "Meghan if I had a son I'd want him to be like you. You're the bestest love," in his soft commanding voice.

We'd wrestle because I'd say he was getting soft headed in his old age and for a while he'd make me work before letting me win. Then he'd fall asleep, his snore sounding like a chainsaw.

Chainsaw?

My head jerked up. I hadn't meant to fall asleep. I snatched off my gloves and pulled out the pistol. Those weren't chainsaws; they were snowmobiles that were still off a ways yet. I rushed to bundle the remaining gear that I hadn't burned before scrambling out into the open ditch as the engines grew closer.

Slipping off the gloves again I tried to find the source of the engines while gripping the gun in my pocket. They were heading my way, apparently following and obscuring my tracks.

Six snowmobiles and a side by side UTV.

I stood tense. If they weren't friendly I wouldn't be able to out run them but I'd damn sure have the initiative. I took off the ski mask and hood. If they were friendly at least I wouldn't freeze to death.

They slowed to a staggered stop, staring at me through goggles or helmets until one turned off his snowmobile and removed his helmet.

He couldn't have been more than 15 or 16 years old. His pimpled cheeks were round and red from the wind. He had easy going blue eyes and wore a smile he probably practiced in the mirror but hadn't quite grown into yet.

"Howdy, Miss Lady, I'm Shane-"

"Shane this ain't no time for your shameless flirting!" A short brunette with the same eyes and cheeks sans the acne pushed at his shoulder.

"Shucks, Sara Lee, I'm just being neighborly so I don't scare her none."

They all wore hunting gear in various shades of white, grays, and greens. Sara Lee had a customized rifle slung across her back.

She gently took my face in her mittened hands, tsked at either the sight of my face or my wince, and studied me as if we'd known each other our entire lives. Then she led me to the passenger side of the UTV and sat me inside. I placed my pack on my lap as she pointed past me.

"This is Duke, he won't bother you none. You look like you're done in so you get some rest before we get to town. Duke give this poor girl some of your hot chocolate before she freezes to death."

Duke was a square dude; cinderblock jaw, wide shoulders, fingers like rolls of quarters. Hazel eyes topped a boxy nose that had been broken a time or two and his skin was freckled and a shade of brown so light he'd have passed as white during slavery times. His voice was deep, solid as a mountain, and his words were slow as a frozen stream.

"Sara Lee has a way taking charge don't leave no question in mind," he said once she closed us in together. He handed me a tall thermos and cautioned. "Just a nip, mind you, there's a quarter of Bailey's mixed with a quarter coco and half French vanilla 'cino."

"Thank you, Duke, but I don't drink alcohol." I was already feeling warmer thanks to the heater blowing on my feet.

Duke pulled goggles down over his eyes before following his crew. He drove in silence for a while then asked if I was allergic to booze.

"Technically no, I just don't like it much."

Another few minutes passed before, "Sara Lee'd be mighty upset if I don't get a lil' warmth in your belly. Will you just take a nip so I can say I done as she asked?"

Not wanting to offend him I took a tiny sip after giving it a good shake. He was right about warmth in my belly. I offered him a few granola bars in exchange. He took two.

"Obliged." He ate both in two bites so I gave him two of the larger protein bars. "These're my favorite. Thank you kindly."

He smiled so long I wondered if he was a little slow. Then again maybe he was a deep thinker. He took a long drink from the thermos which alleviated some of my caution.

I ate a few granolas as I shielded my eyes from the glare of the morning sun off pristine powder.

Duke smacked his thigh and made me jump. "Don't know where my manners went."

He reached up to the roof, not much of a reach for him, where there were a bunch of Velcroed pockets. Reaching into one he pulled out moist lemon towelettes then a pair of sunglasses from another.

"This should help. What's your name anyway?"

"Thanks, I'm Meghan."

"And I'm Duke, officially that is, nice to meet your acquaintance."

"How long before we reach town?" I yawned.

He rubbed his beardless jaw thoughtfully. "Can't rightly say. You see that storm blew out the phone lines and some folks didn't answer their CBs all night. So we took it upon ourselves to check on them at first light if they ain't answered by then.

"Well, old lady Mable still ain't answered. If she's alright it'll depend on how long she squawks. If she ain't...well, we'll see."

By then I'd wiped away all the blood and donned the glasses. The warmth and relative safety made me drowsy. Or maybe that was my concussion being persuasive.

"You like country music?" he asked presently.

Yawn. "Love it."

I pulled out Chopper's cell to check for a signal and sighed when I didn't find one.

"We're too far from the cities to get cell phone services," Duke said apologetically.

Then he turned on a little radio and Kenny Chesney's voice filled the small cab. Duke sang along in a surprisingly pleasing bass. My eye lids suddenly grew too heavy to hold up. I fell asleep to the sweet crooning of Josh Turner and Duke minutes later.

XX

"...poor girl sleep, Lord knows she needs it. Any hoot Mable is squawking so we'll be a while yet."

The comforting words drifted through my foggy mind but I drifted back to sleep. It seemed like only a second passed before Duke was gently shaking my shoulder. My head was pillowed on his thigh. I sat up hastily muttering an apology.

He smiled casually. "I never mind being a pretty girl's pillow."

8:17, nearly two hours sleep. I stretched as much as the cabin allowed and thought of Yoshi. I missed my baby. She was probably yowling for someone to feed her. Poor girl. I couldn't wait to get back.

We pulled into town on the main road, parking in front of a sporting goods store. A glance showed a small grocery store, a small bank, a small sheriff's office, a gas station, and a diner. There were several trucks parked here and there but mostly the street was lined with snow mobiles, ATVs and more UTVs.

I was expecting a camera crew to round the corner following three cannibalistic siblings intent on killing everybody a la Wrong Turn.

"Meghan," Sara Lee called from the door of the sporting goods store, "we should talk before you eat."

She waved me inside while the others laughed and joked as they headed for the diner.

She turned on the lights and turned the dead bolt, keeping the closed sign hanging as it lay. Upon closer inspection I didn't know whether to call it a store or a lodge or something else.

Something else seemed appropriate. Aisles of hunting necessities filled part of the spacious floor directly in front of me. To my right was a wall full of carefully selected camping and cold weather gear, part of which held shelves of men and women's boots like an outback Foot Locker.

To my immediate left a display case held an array of handguns behind which was an array of hunting rifles in a locked rack. Sara lee hung her rifle on two mounted hooks then knelt next to a stone fire place and kindled a fire.

"I don't need to know what happened in that van, Meghan, but I'd say you better get outta their clothes."

She stood, a gravity to her gaze. She couldn't have been more than 19 or 20 but she had the aura of someone used to being obeyed. It didn't take a rocket scientist to know how she deduced I'd been in the van. She, or her entire crew, had probably checked it out of curiosity before running into me.

My only question was, "Why are you helping me?"

Not that I wasn't grateful.

She huffed then hustled me away from the door. "First it was because of my horoscope. You read the horoscope?"

She guided me through the aisles waving a hand at the clothing I could choose from.

"Sometimes," I answered as I searched for what would fit.

"Don't worry about the prices, this is my Ma and Pa's place and it'll be on me." She must've thought my perusal was due to prices. If only.

"No," I denied firmly. "You're doing more than enough already. This is a small town and you'll need my business. Plus I can afford it." I showed her a roll of bills.

"Fine," she conceded, changing subjects. "I'm an Aries. Can you imagine what my horoscope said today?" She guided me around the shop with a critical eye at the items I picked: all practical yet expensive, the best she had to offer.

"Not a clue."

I picked up a pair of insulated waterproof boots that caught my attention. They were white, silver, and gray with pink accents.

"It said 'look outside yourself for answers. Friendship will blossom in the unlikeliest places. Safe harbor is within your power.' Then what am I supposed to think when you come stumbling into the picture bruised and nearly frozen to death?"

Her question was challenging. Not having an answer I asked for the boot in a size 5. She took that as an answer. She took the price tags to the register on the display case. The fire place gave the shop a natural warmth that I soaked up gratefully as I waited.

"Throw that stuff in the flame before you change."

I happily paid before throwing everything but my dress into the flames. We stood there in silence broken only by the crackling flames.

"You said you helped me at first because of your horoscope..." I ventured.

"I also know who you are," she replied softly into the flames. "I recognized you almost immediately."

I hated jumping to conclusions but I looked around anyway expecting a trick. Her gaze was riveted by the flames.

"How?"

"I was young when it happened but I remember my Ma and Pa saying it must take a strong constitution to prevail during a trial like yours. I tore your picture out of a few papers for a school project about heroes. It said 'Meghan Wahlin is my Wonder Woman."

I was shocked, I mean, what do you say to that?

"After seeing that van before recognizing you I thought somebody must of been in trouble."

Her eyes, glimmering with unshed tears, met mine.

"If I think your luck is that bad I'm glad you escaped before anything could happen." Her voice was fierce.

"Thank you."

She squished me in a sudden bear hug, her hair smelling like green apples. She stepped back hastily, smiling self-consciously.

Pointing to the pistol I'd placed on the counter she asked, "You know how to use that?"

"My papa taught me a thing or few." Satisfied her.

She led me to the far left of the shop. There, demarcated by a glass plate wall, was a room with a few wooden tables, checker boards carved into them, and heavy wooden chairs.

Sara Lee pointed to the door. "There's a small bedroom with a shower in there if you wanna clean up."

"Seriously?"

"Yep. It's just an intimate spot my pa built so one of us could have a piece of privacy when needed. I'll go get your boots, now scoot...and take your time 'cause there's plenty of hot water."

CH10

Had I become a magnet for trouble or was it this run?

Honestly the answer eluded me thanks to the omens. How was I supposed to know when I'd cut myself shaving in Sara Lee's rustic shower for the first time in years? How could I know when I dropped her blow dryer on my foot after dark memories of Club Sin flashed through my mind and made my hands tremble?

Then to top it all off there was no way I could contact Motown or Carmen.

I sighed heavily, pulling on my new boots.

Sara Lee's little bedroom was cozy considering how small it was. Her bed touched three walls, big enough for two wild bodies, long enough for a tall guy like Duke to fit comfortably.

There was dark carpeting, a shelf of DVDs and a 30' HD Toshiba.

A sudden crash and feminine cry brought me to my feet in a rush. I grabbed the pistol off the bed beside me, clicked off the safety, then ran out into chaos.

"...is she?"

It was the tail end of a question Sara Lee obviously refused to answer. Her back was pressed against the short side of the display counter. One of the shelves had been pulled down onto its front, glass lay scattered over dark wood like Dalmatian spots.

The man stood between her frantically drumming legs as he choked her. I didn't know who he was but I didn't need to. In the movies the hero usually says something witty and gives away his advantage. I hadn't made a sound but he looked up and our eyes met as if he knew I was standing there. I recognized him immediately.

The third chipmunk gave me an evil grin. He stood, pulling Sara Lee into his thick body as a shield. He put a wicked looking knife to her throat, enough that she whimpered as a scarlet trickle stained her slender neck. Her eyes held fear and doubt.

"I'm not supposed to kill you..." he paused, shrugging dramatically, "but she ain't you."

"Now, you can either drop your gun and come with us and she'll live...or not and she'll die and then you'll come with us..."

Last time I checked I was nobody's dummy but things went too fast for words. If he killed her she'd be dead weight and then I'd kill him. He had to know that even as he droned on about me murdering his relatives.

In the movies the hero always drops the gun after relenting. I hate when they do because it makes no sense. Technicalities aside gun beats knife more than Laura Croft beats tombs. None of which mattered to me in that clarified moment. I knew this battle was lost it was in both their eyes.

His held nothing but victorious gloating.

But some battles are worth fighting.

Both their eyes darted behind me.

My gun barked a split second before my nerves exploded in searing hot pain. I lost all control as a lightning bolt of electricity scrambled every signal I wanted my nerves to receive.

From my newly acquired position on the floor the third chipmunk hollered about his ear. Apparently it had been shot off. Lucky him. I'd missed.

Sara Lee chose that moment to lunge for her rifle.

With a belligerent howl he slammed his blade into her back. Her head arched back in a scream that was only a wheeze from her bruised throat. He hit her again in the side. Blood blossomed like a deadly rose. She fell face first and lay still. Tears rushed unimpeded from my eyes in a torrent I couldn't control.

"Marcus, we need to go."

Marcuse nearly stabbed her again but his cohort's words held his attention. One hand was trying to stem the blood flowing from his ear. I took a perverse enjoyment in that as Taser man secured my wrists and ankles with a zip-tie.

Marcus jury-rigged a bandage before they shouldered me like a throw rug and Taser threatened to tase me until I passed out if I struggled. My curiosity didn't extend to finding out how long that'd take. Thoughts of Sara Lee almost made me say fuck it. Almost. They carried me through a rear exit and threw me in the trunk of a Tahoe or Denali; I couldn't tell which.

Taser taped my mouth with duct tape then slammed the door down in my face.

"I swear I'm gonna fuck that bitch up," Marcus whined once they were settled up front. "That bitch shot half my ear off!"

"It could be worse but there's Vicodin in the glove box."

"Easy for you to say." Proceeded shuffling papers then the tell-tell rattle of bottled pills.

"Don't look at me like you wanna cut my ear off. We all took a risk."

Taser laughed a surprisingly contagious laugh. I thought that was the problem with bad people; they could be so normal. Relatively speaking. In my opinion bad should look bad. You don't see the Wicked Witch dressed like Mariah Carey for Halloween. No, she's just as cruel as she looks. More bad guys should try that.

My heart suddenly leapt as sirens filled the air behind us.

I scraped-shuffled-pushed my way to my knees and caught a glimpse of Marcus unfolding the stock of an M5. Our eyes met. He grinned maliciously. I shivered more than a little because it reminded me so much of Ira.

"I hope they're coming for you, bitch."

I turned away from his vindictive taunt. All the windows were tinted but I made out a Jeep Cherokee with sirens on top. The cop pulled behind us. My stomach dropped. From my position I could see his righteous fury but he had no clue what he was up against. He was driving straight into an ambush with little more than a badge, some courage and the law to protect him, neither of which was bulletproof.

Marcus opened the sunroof, stuck the upper half of his body out, and stitched the hood of the jeep. It swerved, slid a bit in all the snow, but maintained pursuit.

I wished I could slip my hands from behind my back but they'd tied my hands and feet too tightly so with that option unavailable I took what slack I had and toppled over the rear seat. Thankfully Marcus blocked me from his cohort's view.

Marcus whooped.

I looked back to spot the Jeep spin out into a ditch. Smoke poured from the engine block.

Behind the Jeep another truck had been hidden. The new school Suburban made my heart leap with joy. Motown!

I spotted my Subaru pull off towards the Jeep before bullets struck Motown's truck. Bullet proofing prevented any real damage. Marcus's reaction sent fear down my spine. He barked out a laugh then ducked back in and pulled a fresh magazine from the driver's seat pouch then laughed as he loaded it with a slap-snap.

His first barrage slammed into the grill and hood as we hit a bump. One cracked the windshield, forcing Motown to swerve. He was using armor piercing rounds!

I scraped-shuffled-pushed my way across the last barrier between us. I had to try to help any way I could. I slumped over the seat, my legs facing him. Bound as they had me I could only bump him as I lashed out with both feet at his hip.

He fell back into the truck, bracing himself against the door and driver's seat. He batted my next feeble attempt aside with his rifle then laid into my body with it. I curled in on myself and took it just to give my friends a chance.

"Stupid bitch!"

There was little I could do but tense up and accept the first few painful blows. He aimed one at my face but I turned away the best I could.

"Marcus stop!"

The truck jerked sharply enough that he lost his balance.

"Use the chloroform, dammit. You got them off our asses now don't ruin this, you know Martize wants her unharmed."

I wondered why Martize had given such an order even as I thanked heaven for small favors. I had the bad grace to look up and catch Marcus's livid eyes. He delivered a parting blow that actually left me windless.

He disappeared into his seat then returned seconds later with a rag and a bottle. He sat on my bruised belly and was none too gentle as he slapped the rag over my mouth and nose. After the stinging blows I'd just received I couldn't have held my breath if I wanted to. But with terrible thoughts of what might've happened to Motown, Carmen, and the cop I didn't even try to fight the inevitable.

Some battles, after all, aren't worth fighting.

XX

The latest duo took me to the house.

Not a house but literally the house Derrick and Ira had held me captive.

I recognized the living room the second my sleep blurred eyes focused. The furniture was different, newer, a little more modern, but some things you don't forget, can't forget no matter how hard you try. The stylized arch separating the tatty diamond wall paper living room from the salmon kitchen was unmistakable. There were still scratches gouged in the wood by a desperately struggling young woman. I can remember wondering if I'd been the first secured to it or was I just one of many. Thankfully I hadn't woken up in the room, it's the only thing that kept me from freaking out.

Now I was strapped to a steel chair like a death row inmate waiting on his electrocution to commence as I shook off the aftereffects of the chloroform they'd used to knock me out.

"There's no point struggling."

The woman walked hunched over with a hand on her lower back. She wore rectangular tortoise shell glasses that made her black marble eyes seem bigger than robin eggs. Her hair was sliver and her voice just as steely. Her entire demeanor radiated hate.

I didn't bother pleading. Bad ass? Naw, just realistic.

"You killed my baby's." Her breath was redolent of mints when it should've smelled like stale cigarettes and blind maggots. In other words what I considered the smell of evil.

"I didn't ask for any of this."

She slapped me with more force than her thin frame suggested.

"Auntie Gemma."

Martize walked in flanked by Marcus and Taser. I wanted to ask him why or how could he do something like this but he was subtly different somehow. There was a calm demented cast to his posture and a cold glint in his eyes I'd never seen before.

How could someone hide such obvious crazy?

What an actor he turned out to be.

Having the final physical proof that he did have everything to do with this horrible predicament had me just a little shook. Locking eyes with him I felt my heart break. That last little bubble of someone-could-be-framing-him doubt burst like an expired pop rock; sharp and bitter.

He was the first guy I'd given half a chance romantically after the fiasco with his cousins.

Mentally shaking my head I wondered what the odds must be of that happening. He had pressed all the right buttons, had put in all the right codes.

"I trusted you," I couldn't help but blurt out.

That bothered me the most. I'd opened myself up for him, trusted him even when my friends had reservations.

"That was the plan." He smirked.

"I don't know what my baby's saw in you," Gemma scowled, "but you better believe Martize would never like someone like you."

She shuffled over to an oversized chair and sunk down into its stuffed cushions with a sigh.

"Stand her up," Martize ordered his goons.

"Why? What's the point of any of this?"

"Justice!" Gemma shouted. "You killed-"

Martize cut her off with an upheld hand as Taser and Marcus unbound my hands.

"Auntie Gemma never forgave you for killing Derrick and although Ira died in prison, as you know, that was also your fault. Neither would have happened had you not been such a tease."

The duo had me standing by then; each held an arm in vice grips. Martize pulled out a butterfly knife with a flourish. I couldn't think of anything to say. I was too angry.

"It took some time to formulate a plan but I never thought I'd be the one to get you in all honesty."

He took a step towards me. I hated that my legs were still secured to the chair because at least then I could've lashed out at him. Everything I'd heard up until this moment told me he had bigger plans than just killing me out right. Given half the chance I'd fight back before I let them lock me into their dungeon again.

"You turned down a few others I sent at you, after all," he chuckled as he slid the knife into the top of my shirt. He slowly pushed it down, slicing through the thick shirt.

How many of the guys I had turned down had been a part of his plan? I tried focusing on that as he cut my clothes away layer by layer but there was no way to know and nothing could really take my mind off my predicament no matter how hard I tried.

So I raised my chin defiantly. Inside I screamed and hollered.

"Now you boys tell me what so special about her," Gemma demanded. "Is it her breast? Her ass? What's so special that my boy wanted to keep her caged? Which one of you can tell me that!" she asked them all but her eyes were on Martize.

"It wasn't just her body they wanted," he explained. "They wanted to break her. Look how stubborn she is." He placed the tip of his knife against the racing pulse in my throat.

"She thinks she's tough," Martize snarled.

"And so she deserves to be broken," Gemma reasoned.

I once saw a picture on the internet of a bunch of religious fanatics. Every face held the same intense look aimed at me.

"Why now?"

Martize started a laugh that had them joining him like a pack of wild hyenas. He pressed the knife into my breast. I couldn't contain a gasp of pain as a drop of blood welled around the tip of the blade.

"What's my name?"

"Martize Witherspoon," I replied through clenched teeth.

He twisted his blade. "Otherwise known as?"

"Teaser," Preceded moist eyes.

He turned away, laughing. I didn't get the joke.

"Most people think I only tease women in bed but it's much deeper than that. I tease myself as well. All of life becomes a tease in the right circumstances. Take my cousin's house for instance. After you so rudely took his life no one wanted this property to stand. So I was able to buy it dirt cheap and relocate it.

"That," he pointed at me with his blade, "is only part of 'why now.' I needed to tease myself and those apart of my plan."

"I wasn't a fan of delayed gratification when this began," Marcus told him. "I'm still not convinced it's worth it."

He leered at my body and I berated myself for trembling when he smiled at my reaction. I didn't think I could go through another tragedy and come out sane on the other side. I didn't want to be trapped in that windowless room entertaining their every whim.

"But this became the perfect time," Martize continued. "You refused to back off the run as I expected you would. Now anybody who asks will think you came up missing because of your run."

Revenge is all I heard in his self-deluded spill. That confused me. Wasn't he...

"That's all good," Taser said, "but let's not forget about the dough."

Martize stepped chest to chest with him. His voice went soft. Dangerous.

"Do you think I've forgotten the plan Keiser?"

Keiser didn't flinch. "The fact is, Martize, you're acting like a movie villain revealing your grand plan like it matters. Remember why some of us joined you."

They stared at each other for so long I wished my legs were free so I could at least try escaping. The front door was less than 20 feet away. It might as well have been Pluto.

Martize finally said, "There's one thing we must do."

He turned to me before patting Keiser patronizingly on the shoulder. When he stopped his chest was mashed against mine.

"Where's the package, Meghan?"

"She'll never tell us without the proper convincing," Marcus suggested.

"That's not true at all," I said. "I have no interest in the package now that it's been delivered."

He moved faster than I could react, punching me in the solar plexus, and only the duo holding me upright kept me from falling over sideways as the wind rushed out of me with a pained grunt.

"You never had a chance to finish your run," he said.

"When's the last time you saw me in a club?" I wheezed to his back.

"Hit her again for her impertinence. I don't want to hear her talking back," Gemma ordered.

He spun back around, landing another blow to my solar plexus that made me gag.

"Now get her out of my sight," Gemma said.

They pulled my hands behind my back roughly before Martize cut my feet free. He walked ahead of us as Gemma taunted me from behind.

"Hope you enjoy yourself, bitch."

As they forced me down that hallway I felt like I was walking the green mile. I had done my best not to panic up till this moment but when I saw that door with my name on it like I was some kind of star I panicked.

Martize turned to say something but met my foot with his nuts. As he bent I landed a snap kick to his chin. He fell over backwards but I knew he wasn't out by a long shot.

I aimed a kick at Marcus's knee but he dodged. They simultaneously tensed to pick me up by the armpits so I jumped, flipping over to break their grips. I wasn't going to get away, I knew it, but that didn't stop me from lashing out. I would do absolutely anything, even get myself killed, to avoid going back into that room.

Marcus blocked my next kick then rushed me. He picked me up around the waist, I pulled my feet up anticipating the following slam into the wall. What surprised me was when my feet went through it as we collided with it.

Gemma screamed something but I was too occupied to understand what it was.

Marcus pulled away. I elbowed his chin then wrapped my hands around the back of his neck to keep my balance. He caught me with an uppercut to the body then the chin. I let go as stars swam in my eyes and slumped onto the floor face first, feet stuck in the wall.

Keiser tased me. It went on for what felt like forever before it suddenly stopped.

I heard an explosion. Screams. I caught a glimpse of Martize running away.

Running away?

I got my head around with effort and thought I was hallucinating.

Motown, Carmen, and some other guy, were sweeping into the house like Call of Duty black ops. There were no questions asked, no orders given. Marcus and Keiser were shot where they stood. Gemma screamed obscenities before a shot went off to silence her.

Motown pulled me free from the wall.

"Did I crash your party?"

I smiled even as my chin trembled. Then I burst out crying.

CH11

Carmen took one glowering look at me before kicking Marcus then sweeping past with the cop behind her.

"We'll search," he told Motown. "Take care of her."

He nodded but his attention was already focused on me. He tenderly wrapped his coat around my nakedness and checked the wound on my neck. He bandaged it while asking;

"What hurts, Meghan?"

I looked around and slid down the wall. There were tears in my eyes and a hitch in my chest that threatened to overwhelm me. I needed to get out of the house before I was swamped by memories.

I huddled in the coat while swiping at my eyes. "How did you find me?"

"As long as you were wearing the rose pendant you were never lost."

"Are you serious, you put a tracker on me?"

I believed it in that I can't believe it kind of way. I stared into his soulful brown eyes and wondered why I was the only one who hadn't put faith in him. Eric would have every right to say I told you so.

"You're welcome," he said.

Carmen returned with the cop. I recognized him from the Jeep once he stood in front of me. He was older up close with cropped gray hair and a gray goatee. He had a shotgun resting on a thick waist.

"Are you ok?" Carmen asked.

I shrugged, not trusting any other answer. "Are you ok officer? I saw you run off the road."

He shook his head. "I don't think I'll ever be ok after what they did to my sister."

"You're Sara Lee's brother?"

"Albert Lee." He offered a hand to shake. "I'll wait for you outside."

"Aren't you going to call this in?" I asked while shaking his hand.

"I have no jurisdiction here and explaining this would be a nightmare." His eyes suddenly gleamed with tears. "They killed my sister. They can rot here for all I care."

"I'm so sorry." He turned and walked out without another word.

"So what now?" Carmen asked after a moment of silence.

"Why did they bring you here?" Motown asked.

"Because this is the house Ira and Derrick held me captive..." I explained everything I knew.

"Martize managed to escape," Carmen sighed.

"We should torch this place," I said viciously.

We all looked at one another for a moment and came to a silent agreement. 15 minutes later we were sitting in Motown's truck as the house blazed like Zeus's first bonfire. Sheriff Hemps worth told me how he'd gotten involved through a silent alarm at Sara Lee's shop.

I wanted to cry for the girl who'd given her life to help a stranger. I held off until I was in the back seat of Motown's truck. There were plenty of tears. Some were even for me.

XX

Sara Lee's brother offered us the use of his house but we declined and ended up at a motel back in Minnesota.

I rode beside Motown in his Suburban while Carmen took my Subaru. We drove in silence even when I stared at him for long periods of time. He held my hand and that compassionate touch was more soothing and comforting than anything anyone could have said.

I focused on that as I stood under the steaming shower spray in my motel room: Motown's comforting touch.

He'd saved me from a fate that could've left me permanently damaged mentally if it didn't leave me dead. He'd risked his life for me. A ton of what ifs ran through my mind before Carmen's voice interfered.

"If if was a spliff we'd all be high as Bob Marley."

I just wanted to get out of my own head and forget all about the troubles I'd gone through So after dressing in a white shirt and matching chiffon skirt and navy blue leggings I threw on my coat, a pair of flats and made my way down to Motown's room. He greeted me without a shirt on and up tempo R&B

playing in the back ground. His skin was covered by a sheen of sweat that steamed in the evening chill.

"Hey," I said as I second guessed myself.

"Hey yourself."

"Can we...talk?"

"Absolutely."

He waved me into the room. His spicy scent permeated the air like a baker's kitchen. He'd moved the bed to the far wall and put down a square's worth of towels that were obviously damp.

"Did I interrupt your workout?"

He shrugged. "Just doing katas. So what do you wanna talk about, Meghan?"

"What're you listening to?" I asked to avoid answering.

I think he knew why I was here but was waiting on me to make up my mind or encourage him to make the first move. Understandable considering how many times I'd been the SAM to his F-15 and shot him down.

"A track I've been working on."

He closed the distance and removed my coat, throwing it into a corner chair without breaking eye contact. He took my hands, put them both around his neck then serenaded me as he rocked us back and forth.

"Don't over think it, this ain't rocket science. Your lips say you don't want it, but your body says you're lying. I can feel... the chemistry. And the way your heart is beating, it's like you ran straight into me."

I smiled on the outside even as I swooned on the inside. "How can you not believe in happenstances at times like this?"

"Some things are meant to happen."

"Is this meant to help me forget?" I asked, laying my cheek on his chest.

He tilted my chin until our eyes met.

"I can't promise you'll forget but I'll give you something better worth remembering."

"Promise?" I whispered.

His answer was a slow tender kiss that started out all lips and nips but ended with just enough tongue to make me moan and appreciate his sensual skill. He pushed me back against the bed but turned so that he sat and I stood.

"Your moan is incredible," he murmured as he did that you don't have clothes on touch.

I bit my lip as his hands found my breasts and his soft lips brushed over my belly right above the waistband of my leggings. His touch was gentle yet insistent. Not until that moment did I realize it was exactly what I needed; someone who could guide without being overbearing.

I pulled my shirt off. Motown smiled as if he'd been waiting on me to do just that. His smile was so sincere and sexy I turned my back to him, dipped it low, and pulled off the leggings.

"Damn," he growled before squeezing my ass.

I moaned in surprise and delight.

"You don't know how much I've wanted to do that, Meghan."

I turned back to him, watched him drink me in, then asked, "What else have you wanted to do?"

"Kiss you until your knees buckle," he murmured while pulling me closer.

"Oh joy."

Our lips tangled and there was no hesitance between us. There was nothing but lips, pants, and thrills. His fingers skimmed over my skin which was growing hotter with each caress. His muscles were hard beneath my hands.

I broke the kiss to taste his skin, moving from his lips to his ear to his neck.

"Hmm," he moaned.

So I gave him another kiss to the same spot. He rewarded me by sliding his hand between my waiting nana and making me gasp. He palmed me, grinding his hand against my clit until I rocked on it of my own accord. Then he slid off the bed and sat between my legs, looking up at me with a cocky grin.

"I love how wet you are."

"Kiss my thighs, Motown."

He suckled each in turn until my toes tingled and I knew there'd be hickies there in the morning. My back arched when his tongue split my lips and he began to keep his promise. I don't know how he did it but between one smooth lick and another his swirling tongue began to vibrate around my clit. My legs began to tremble.

"Motown."

He was perfect, sliding two fingers inside me while matching the pace of his tongue. My eyes closed in pleasure. I was starting to believe he actually could make my knees buckle because I could feel my climax building faster than it ever had before. His tongue continued to wreak havoc on my motor functions as his fingers grew slicker with each upward plunge into my body in perfect synchronicity. He grabbed my ass with his free hand and with a firm squeeze pushed me over the edge.

"Ooh joooy," I panted as I sank onto his lap with his help.

My entire body vibrated and tingled with the rush of my climax. I laid my head on his shoulder to wait it out but he was far from done with me. He fed me my own juices with his tongue as he lifted me up to slowly slide me onto his erection. So slowly I came again with one soft inhale that broke our kiss.

"You're so tight," he moaned. He sounded surprised. "Take what you need, Meghan."

I could hardly think past the depth and pressure of him inside me. He stretched and filled me as if we were made for each other. Still I managed a questioning gaze.

"You need this more than you want it so take what you need."

His insight was astounding but his compassion was overwhelming. Everything about him said he wanted me but he wanted me to be happy first. He was a strong powerful man and could've easily taken control of this encounter. Instead he was giving me the reins.

He was giving me the choice.

He'd wanted me for years and yet there was no urgency in his caresses. That was humbling and sexy as hell. It made me more comfortable than I'd ever been with a guy. It made me want to exorcise all my demons and forget all my fears.

"I trust you," I told him.

There were so many things he could've said but he didn't say anything. I found that the best thing he could've said because his responding kiss was so much more potent than any words. Besides, the man could kiss so well my toes curled as I wrapped my legs around his waist. Taking his hands I placed them firmly on my ass.

"Move me slowly, Motown."

I expected something simple. What I received took my breath away. He pulled me to him, raised me up his shaft, pushed me backwards and lowered me all in one smooth motion. I laid my forehead against his as he kept up that fantastic Ferris wheel motion.

"Wow that feels good, Motown."

He moaned an affirmative, working hard to maintain the pace. The angle changes brought me closer to a new climax. I added a thrust when his arms began to tremble that made us both gasp.

"Don't stop... I'm close... please don't stop..." I pleaded.

He sped up, lowered me a little harder and thrust simultaneously causing us both to cry sharply. Our moans mingled with each thrust. I threw my head back as my climax hit. Motown latched onto a nipple and every tingle, tremble and moan multiplied.

There was absolutely no hiding how amazing he had me feeling.

He pulled me down, held me there, and let his moan fill the room as he came.

"Meghan Meghan Meghan..."

I took my legs back and rolled off him. He pulled off his condom as I stood on shaky legs. He'd made me vulnerable and I needed to go.

"Stay, Meghan."

I debated it for a split second. He'd given me more than any man ever had. There was only my own reservations preventing me from staying but he wasn't going to pressure me. I knew that now.

"I need a shower."

"I'll join you."

He didn't need to convince me to stay, but he did.

CH12

I woke up with Motown spooned behind me, his breath soft against the nape of my neck while another part was hard and ready against my ass. I wouldn't tell him but I completely understood how he earned his reputation.

It's safe to say that if I didn't actually forget all of my trouble I certainly had enough to think about during dark moments...or any other moment the mood struck.

He suddenly hugged me to him and kissed my neck gently. Chills traced my spine from his lips.

"Morning," he said with that heavy sleep laden voice.

"How'd you know I was awake?" I hadn't moved an inch.

"Your breathing changed."

I turned to him, he pulled my leg over his and intertwined our fingers. The gesture made me forego the sarcastic remark that tipped my tongue.

I pulled away until we weren't touching and frowned.

"I can't be your girl, Motown."

He sighed heavily; resignation transformed his handsome features. "I know."

"What do you mean "I know,' Motown?"

"We got a good thing starting right now that's been a long time in the making."

I started to interrupt but he held up a hand to forestall my rebuttal.

"Let's be honest, Meghan. You want a good man who has a good head on his shoulders, right?"

"Yeah."

"You want a good man who is financially secure, right?"

"Yeah."

"You want a man who is good to his woman, correct?"

"Yeah."

"You also want a man who is respectful, caring and in your own words it wouldn't hurt if he had a big dick and was good in bed, right? Didn't you say all that?"

"Yeah. I did but that doesn't mean..."

"I know what it means, Meghan. It means I'm not finsta sit here and argue with you when I already know where your car is heading. We both know I'm all of that but you're not ready for another titled relationship. So there's no reason to argue about how "I know", Meghan. Just don't expect me to rush anything between us when I don't have to."

"So what do you expect to happen now? Where do we go from here?" It was hard to argue with that kind of confidence and logic.

"I expect to keep things simple until you're ready. Other than that," he stood, yawned, stretched and headed for the bathroom, "we finish this run."

XX

Despite Motown and Carmen's objections I decided to go home. I wished Domeer would try to penalize me for a delay after what I'd just gone through on his behalf so I could tell him off properly. Besides, I missed Yoshi.

Motown decided to come in with me while Carmen stayed with the cars just in case. Yoshi came streaking out of nowhere and leapt into Motown's chest. He caught her on pure reaction as she turned and hissed at a puppy chasing her. It was gray and had floppy ears as big as it was.

"How cuuute," I admired as I picked up the yipping fur ball who immediately attacked my face with kisses.

He wore a collar which read "Kewa." No sooner had I pulled him away from my face and read it than a little ponytailed doe eyed girl ran up to us crying for her puppy. I put her at around 10 years old.

"Kewa, I told you not to chase that cat," she scolded.

"It's ok sweetheart, he didn't hurt her," Motown soothed.

"Are you sure, mister?"

Motown ran a hand over Yoshi's body and nodded. "Yes, she's just fine. She was probably a little faster than Kewa expected huh?"

"Yes." She nodded enthusiastically.

I gave her back her puppy and we sent her on her way a few minutes later. Yoshi stayed curled up in Motown's arms, purring as if she hadn't just been chased by a hellhound. I scratched her ears as we made our way inside. Motown tried handing her off but she clung to him with a yowl.

"I guess all the pussies love you," I said dryly.

He just grinned characteristically and led the way inside. I don't know what he saw but he let Yoshi down as he pulled a pistol from behind his back. He took a step back out of the door and turned to me.

"Wait here," he ordered softly.

I waited, but I watched for anyone suspicious until he returned.

"You and Carmen aren't gonna like what you find inside."

I took a few steps around him until I reached the living room. It was wrecked.

"The entire place is like that," Motown said as I took in the damage.

Someone had been searching for something. It looked like the police had executed a search warrant on a poor person's house.

"Do you think Martize did this?"?

"I wouldn't discount it but I don't see a reason why he'd go through the effort."

"He tore up everything though, Motown." My voice cracked.

He hugged me from behind. "It's nothing that can't be replaced."

I shook him off. "It's everything that can't be replaced! He violated my personal space.

"Again! How am I supposed to be strong and deal with all of this when I don't have any sense of security left?"

He turned me to him and locked our gazes. "You have your life, your family and you have me, none of this materialistic shit matters in the least, Meghan: it can all be replaced."

"It can't be replaced," Motown. "You can't replace memories. How am I gonna replace the last game my dad bought me? Or the last movie we watched together? How am I gonna replace that, huh? You see all this and think it's just a bunch of replaceable materialistic shit when it all meant something to me. I can't replace the first Sega I ever bought with my own money or..." I just couldn't argue over this.

I looked around at the destruction but was all cried out. Yoshi came and brushed my leg before yowling and heading back towards the kitchen. She just sauntered past everything with her tail held high.

"See, Yoshi knows what's important," Motown said.

I know he did it to lighten the mood but as I toed away broken electronics, couch cushions and broken cabinet drawers I couldn't help but feel anger rising. Yoshi gave me a disapproving yowl when I slammed her water dish down and water slopped over the side.

"Can you tell me what you know about optical computers?"

"They're supposed to be theoretical," I said after a moment's hesitation. "Why are you asking about theoretical computers?"

"Well, long story short, we're carrying a necessary component for it and, while I don't know which component, Domeer has offered us a substantial bonus if we decide to pick up another component. So, again, what can you tell me?"

"Are you trying to verify what he told you?"

"Partially."

I wanted to go into my room and change clothes but I didn't want to wade into the mess.

"Aren't you curious what the bonus is?"

I sighed. "No, this is some bullshit and I'm just wondering how you can stay so calm." I picked up one of my favorite Kenny Chesney CDs and threw the half disk at a wall. Motown stayed where he was by the wall.

"On the inside I'm boiling and when I catch Martize he'll feel my wrath; until then, being angry will only cause me unnecessary stress."

"But how can you stand there and be so calm?" I kicked a ripped cushion his way. I wanted him to feel my anger, to show me the hate he had for Martize on his face.

"If Carmen were here we'd be tearing shit up even worse. There's no way you can think you know me if you don't understand my anger."

"Come here."

I stood at my kitchen sink and stared at him. Yoshi ate her wet food contently by my feet. He waited patiently as if he knew I would go to him.

"Who do you think you're talking to? You think you can just order me around all of a sudden?" I picked up a lamp pole and stared him down. His eyes made me second guess starting a fight with him. They smoldered in a way I'd never seen before as if the carefree guy I knew had vanished.

"Come here, please."

His voice remained calm and that scared me more than anything. Most people looked, acted, sounded angry, but here he stood with a bitch-I-wish-you-would look in his eyes talking as calm as an ocean breeze.

"You think "please" makes a difference?"

"Usually, but you're just looking to start a fight that's unnecessary. I'm on your side."

"Motown, you're too damn calm!"

The pole flew from my hands across the room, a wall received a new hole or two as decoration, a whirlwind of anger exploded until I was all tuckered out and sweaty then I finally flopped down on the kitchen floor, hanging my head between my knees. Hard to believe everything I owned had come through hard work and was now all trash. My Xbox was shattered, my PSP was stuck in a wall, and my PS3 was cracked like a lobster's shell. All of the other electronics I'd stocked up on, ribbons that I'd won in school, original art Carmen and I had worked on, the pillow my dad and I use to share on stormy nights was gone.

Motown came to me, leaving very little space between us without touching me.

"All your shit's fucked up and somebody has to pay. I get that. You can fight me if you want and it'll ease some of your stress but the person who fucked you over is still out there so your anger is bound to return.

"If calm is what you want, the first thing to do is breathe. Then you get out of whatever space is pissing you off by either thinking about something happier or calmer or you talk about something you like.

"Now will you breathe with me?"

"I don't wanna breathe, Motown."

"Can a computer really compute at the speed of light?"

"Theorectically."

"Can a computer really use light instead of electricity?"

"Where did this topic come from all of a sudden?"

"Domeer had called us to his club to tell us what we were risking our asses over and the only thing I could find on optical computing referred to chips and computers that replaced their internal wiring with optical waveguides and some kind of optical transistor that's controlled by photons instead of electrons."

"That's about the gist of it," I agreed once we were back in the hallway. I locked the door behind us and refused to look back.

"Problem is, that's not what Domeer told me."

We stopped just shy of the outside door, looking out the double panes.

"So what did he tell you?"

"Something about lasers, crystals, matrix multiplication, blah blah technical blahbitty blah blah. I didn't quite understand."

I smiled at him. "Are you telling me Motown doesn't know it all?"

"When did Motown make that claim? I'm not the internet, Meghan, I don't know everything."

"Well, from what I understand optical computers won't be possible until 2015 or so, if then, but basically it goes something like this.

"There's a low-power laser that's directed through a liquid crystal grid. The grid is full of pixels that're affected by electricity which in turn affect the laser. After the laser passes through the grid it's picked up by a receiver that analyzes the beam's diffraction and Fourier optics, matrix multiplication and Fourier transforms can then be combined to perform complex maths."

"That sounds about right. He also said something about it consuming very little power and having multiple grids in sequence or parallel."

"That's what makes optical computing so revolutionary. In a normal computer chip most things happen sequentially with each transistor working mostly in serial. But optical computers use every liquid crystal pixel as a processing core, or transistor, and the laser hits every pixel simultaneously-"

"Which means it can make hundreds or thousands of computations at the speed of light?"

"Theoretically it could perform millions."

"Which makes it worth millions."

"Apparently."

CH13

Motown's phone rang as we stood there contemplating the possibilities of a super computer that people were willing to kill over. He answered, listened, then handed me his phone.

"It's for you."

"Hello?"

""I'm happy to learn that your rescue was successful. I hope you weren't severely injured?"

"You gotta lotta nerve calling me," I snarled.

His voice was still every bit as dark and sinister as living tar but Motown's earlier mention of a new commission gave me pause. Still, I didn't believe he was worried about me any more than he would if I'd been a blade of wilting grass.

"Your resourcefulness and resilience has intrigued me."

"Why should I care?"

"I'd like to entrust you with another package."

"And why, after all me and my friends have been through, would I want to do that?"

"Because you have proven yourself capable of handling anything and I'm offering you 15 thousand dollars."

15... thousand... dollars? A girl could do a lot with that kind of money. Motown hadn't been lying when he said I could fix everything if I accepted.

"And what would I have to do exactly?"

"Pick up another package and deliver it to the same place as your current package."

"Will I be shot at, chased, kidnapped or attacked in any way?"

"I'm sure you are completely capable of handling anything that might arise."

"I want 30 thousand." Because he was basically verifying everything I'd said.

Motown's eyebrows shot up at my audacity. Croft's panties if I was going to go back onto the battlefield I should at least try to negotiate. Then he smiled at my challenging expression while giving his signature shrug.

"That can be arranged. Now, are you ready for the particulars?"

"Sure. Just as soon as I get verification that I've been paid."

He wired me the entire 30"on good faith" and we talked.

XX

It felt good being back in the driver's seat after my recent events. Very few people would disagree that feeling in control is great and I'd even add it feels even greater after losing all control.

It took us next to no time to reach Minneapolis where it seems every other car is a box Chevy, Regal, or the occasional Range Rover. We wound up over North, home of drug dealers, shootouts, and gangbangers.

I was even more on alert.

We drove through a few plowed streets as we cased the surrounding blocks around our destination. My second circuit around Motown parked at a random curb so he'd be less conspicuous. Seeing nothing suspicious or alarming I dialed my new contact on a throw away we'd picked up on the way over.

"Who dis?"

His "name" was Marc Jacob but I was not about to call him that.

"Naq," I replied. "I'm here for a pick up."

"Where you at?" Man of few words.

"Outside." Two could play that game.

"What you pushing?"

I pictured him in a window taking a mental inventory of every new vehicle on his block.

"A sky blue Subaru."

He grunted an affirmative then said, "Pull into the alley, stop at the fourth house."

I drove around as instructed. The split level duplex had a wooden stair-balcony combo leading up to the second level. There was a Malibu parked face out on what might've been a lawn in the summer.

A muscular black guy stepped onto the balcony with a large suitcase. He wore big shades, a Pelle Pelle coat and black Timbs. In the middle of a Minne-snowta winter he was shirtless with his coat wide open and I couldn't help but wonder if his mother ever told him about catching pneumonia. Although I couldn't see his eyes, nervousness was evident in the continuous swivel of his head. He skipped down two or three steps in his rush to get to me.

I unlocked the door after readying the hidden Taser in the passenger's seat. It's like one of those massage chairs save for a major dose of high electricity. It's my fail-safe, because shooting someone is...messy. This way I'd have an ace in my sleeve if Muscleman, or any client, wanted the proverbial upper hand.

Don't worry, Carmen has told me a thousand times if she's told me once how passive aggressive I'm being. I just shrug and say whatever works.

I pulled out a clipboard that'd verify my delivery as Muscleman tossed his heavy suitcase on my back floor. He turned back to his house, forcing me to honk my horn. He stopped and turned but didn't return when I waved at him.

I stepped out of my car's relative safety. "Hey, you need to sign the receipt." I waved it for his benefit.

"I don't sign shit," he grumbled as he looked me and the clipboard over and apparently found us lacking. He was my height but twice as broad. Close up he looked like a neck-less bull.

He probably only respected other men on steroids with Mini Cooper keys for privates.

"You don't sign I leave the package sitting on this lot." My gray eyes told him I wasn't afraid because I'd dealt with worse than him.

He picked up my pen. Smart guy.

Revving engines drew our attention to either end of the alley.

"Oh shit," he swore, eyes wide, looking from my car to his porch and weighing his options.

My priorities clear I snatched my clipboard and sank back into my car. Muscleman dropped beside me. Whatever. I thought about trying to chicken my way out of the alley for all of a second before a bullet smacked into my windshield. I was so tired of being shot at and I couldn't help but wonder where Martize was getting all this help from.

In the rearview I noticed a tiny slip of a driveway or what would've been had the houses not been so close. I could probably squeeze through. I hoped so.

Reverse came without a second thought and I swung around to line myself up with the space. One of the oncoming Crown Vics barely missed me. It slid to a stop and a guy in all black jumped out swinging a big pistol-grip shotgun. I ignored the muzzle flash but Muscleman ducked as I crashed through a chain linked fence.

Thank God for bullet-proof glass.

I had just enough speed to whip a J-turn on someone's front lawn. I crashed through a snowman and winced.

"Sorry Frosty."

"Oh shit." Must've been Muscleman's mantra though totally relevant. One of the Crown Vics was forcing its way through my makeshift tunnel. I shot off a curb and down the street after barely splitting between two parked cars.

I slid around a corner, throwing Muscles out of his seat.

"Oh shit!" he cried while grabbing at anything solid and fussing with his seatbelt.

"That tends to happen when people are shooting at me." I zipped into an alley hoping to double my lead only to find it T-boned out. The Crown Vic fishtailed behind me as I downshifted and picked a turn at random, dumping us back onto a main street.

A sharp right slammed Muscles into his door, still fumbling with his 5 point harness.

"Shit, I should've run."

"I can always let you out at the next corner senor ungrateful."

So saying I whipped another right. Passive aggressive? Who me? My radar detector beeped and I instinctively downshifted. Somewhere ahead of me a cop was waiting to bust any speeding motorist he could catch. Blinker on, I made a left onto a side street, eased into another alley then reversed into someone's garage. I don't know who leaves their garage open but I wasn't complaining.

I called Carmen but her phone went to voicemail. Motown answered.

"Where are you?" Concern under lay his calm.

"Safe. You?"

"On my way back to JT's. I T-boned one of the fords as it came through the houses. Neat trick by the way."

"Queen of improv!" Carmen hollered.

"Glad to know you weren't hurt," Motown assured me.

"It's mutual," I replied, "but it's not for their lack of trying." I turned a baleful glare Muscleman's way.

"I don't know nothing," he protested.

His denial didn't make me not want to press the tase-his-ass button any less.

"Pick us up-fuck!"

There was a loud bang and all I could hear was Carmen screaming and the unmistakable sound of gunfire and curses.

I frantically pulled out of the garage and headed back towards JTs shop in the hopes of finding them before anything bad could happen. The gunshots rang through my phone so I lowered my window in an attempt to hear if I was close.

"Shorty what you doing?"

"Ssh." I strained to hear anything over his heavy breathing.

"Ey, who you-"

Whatever he was about to say I cut it off as a cop car forced me to stop at a red light.

"Get out of my car."

"What bitch?"

Made me go off on his ass in Spanish. Who did he think he was talking to? He had a lot of nerve talking to me that way.

"Don't be talking Mexican at me."

I was no longer in a mood to deal with his shit so I pressed the tase-his-ass-button. He jerked and squealed for 10 seconds as I treated his ass for calling me a bitch. I didn't have time to deal with his shit as my friends were getting attacked. The cop across the street suddenly flicked on his cherries and pulled away.

"Get out of my car," I told Muscles the second he stopped twitching.

He began to stutter something but I pushed his shoulder.

"Get out!"

He fumbled for the door before flopping out into the street. I pulled off without a second glance, made an illegal U-turn and followed the cop. We headed a bit east before swinging back north. The road was being managed by a signaling cop ahead but I still managed to see Motown's truck on its side.

The only consolation was that the passenger door was open and even from where I sat the truck was empty. An f-350 with a snow plow was pinned in on the front but was also empty. I drove around the carnage at the first gap in traffic.

They couldn't have gotten far so I drove around in concentric circles hoping beyond hope that I could find one of them. My phone rang with an unfamiliar number. I answered it only because of the situation.

"Meghan," Motown wheezed into the phone. "I'm at a store on 26th and Emerson; I need you to come get me."

"Are you hurt? Where's Carmen?"

"Where are you?"

I looked up at the signs to pinpoint my location as I typed those street names into my GPS.

"Broadway and Lyndale?" I answered, following the GPS directions.

"I'll be waiting for you, just keep your eyes open for Martize."

The second I pulled up to the store Motown limped out to me.

"What hurts, Motown?"

"Never mind that, now, I'll be fine. It's Carmen that I'm worried about."

"Where is she?"

"They took her."

"Tell me what happened."

"We were broadsided on our way to JT's and since my truck was already damaged there was nothing I could do about it. We were able to shoot two of them but they were armored and prepared for us. They broke into my truck and snatched Carmen before leaving a message;

"Meet Martize in Eden Prairie." He stared at me with a deadpan expression that sent chills down my back.

"He doesn't want her Motown."

"I know, but I'm not going to give you to him."

"Motown, you're hurt and Carmen is probably in no better shape. What do you expect me to do?"

"I expect you to call for back up."

"There's no time for that."

"There's absolutely time. He doesn't know that you found me yet, probably didn't expect you to find me for a little while; if at all. Time is of the essence but there's no point giving yourself up to him without a plan."

"Of course not, but if he doesn't kill me outright then we should be able to get her back."

"If he doesn't kill you outright? Are you listening to yourself?"

"He has this thing about delayed gratification and I don't think he has reached the end of his plan yet."

Motown grimaced but he was in no position to argue with me. Carmen was in danger; there was no way I wouldn't give myself up to save her.

"At least let me get some more fire power," he finally conceded.

I wasn't going to argue with him on that.

CH14

When we made it to Jt's Motown was wincing and breathing shallowly. I hadn't even noticed he was hurt until the garage doors closed behind us. He was gripping his ribs but there was no blood so his grimace still worried me.

"Motown, I thought you said you weren't hurt."

"I'll be fine."

JT and I helped him into the garage despite his objections. JT took a few minutes to check him over before concluding;

"They're probably fractured," JT concluded.

I looked on as he began to bandage Motown's ribs, even through a wince he managed to bluff.

"No way of telling without an x-ray, fam, but for now I can function."

Before I could reproach him for being so stubborn his cell phone rang. Our eyes locked when we realized it was Carmen's ringtone. He answered on speaker.

"Hello?"

"Don't sound too happy to hear from me, Motown," Martize gloated. "But it's all good, I never liked you anyway."

"Where are Carmen and Meghan?" He surprised me by asking.

"Funny you should ask. You see, Carmen is of no use to me dead and Meghan is the one I want so you tell her that if I don't hear from her within the hour...well you were a soldier once, use your imagination." With that he disconnected.

My heart was trying to break out of my chest as I imagined what he had done, or was doing, to Carmen as she waited for us to rescue her. I groaned as I bent with my hands on my knees. Flashbacks began to bombard me as my imagination started running wild, putting Carmen in my place, and I began to watch her endure the pain that I had.

A huge sob tore its way out of my throat.

"Don't touch her, JT!" Motown barked before his voice penetrated my thoughts.

"Meghan, please stay here. We need you right now, Carmen needs you. I need you. We don't know what she's going through but we can certainly make sure it doesn't last because he fucked up. He gave us time and Carmen was still wearing her rose pendant when I saw her last.

We can find her before he's ready for us.

The hope in his voice broke through my fears; his gentle words brought me back from the brink of despair. I sniffled a few times and raised watery eyes to his sincere brown orbs. There was strength enough for us both in his eyes. I latched onto that strength and gathered myself after a few final sniffles.

"I'm sorry, Motown, it's just-"

He embraced me. "I know, Ma, it's hard dealing with what you've been through."

He got us both to our feet, wiping my face with his shirt.

"Get us some gear," he told Jt.

"Got it."

"Meanwhile, you and me are gonna locate Carmen's pendant."

He took me to his truck where he grabbed a laptop from the trunk. He sat on the edge of the trunk, eyeing me steadily.

"Meghan, you don't have to go through this alone anymore," he said when he turned and caught my worried expression. "I can only imagine the horror you went through with them but I know PTSD when I see it. If you think it'll be better to sit this out I'll fully support your decision. But know that if you continue it's only gonna get harder as you face the worse enemy of your life. I'll be here supporting you through that, too, but nothing's gonna help if you don't or can't support yourself.

"So tell me now, what do you wanna do?"

I turned away from him.

I hadn't been this vulnerable in years. Sure certain sounds or images could trigger a flashback but I thought all of that was behind me. Apparently not as much as I wanted it to be.

The struggle I was having now was real; it could compromise other's safety.

Did I want to risk someone else's life? Or could I deal with the images swirling around in my head? I knew there wouldn't be an immediate solution to the problem but I had been stronger than the assholes in life so why couldn't I be stronger than them in death?

Why did I have to let their memories haunt me when I hated them so much? Croft's panties I didn't.

I shouldn't.

I wouldn't.

I might not get over Martize's betrayal for some time but Carmen and Motown shouldn't have to suffer for my lack of focus. I was stronger than them then and by my papa's spirit there was no way I wouldn't be stronger than them now.

Motown was busy on his laptop when I turned back around but I knew he'd be listening and deserved an honest answer.

"I don't know how I'll react to certain stimuli moving forward but there's no way I'm gonna let Carmen suffer because I was having a nervous breakdown. I've never been weak and I don't like feeling weak now so if you'll have me I want to help.

Looking up he grabbed the front of my shirt, pulled me close, and kissed me before I knew it. Just as suddenly he released me.

"That's all any of us can ask for."

I stood there with my mouth gaping as JT walked past us to the garage door.

"Gear's here."

A matching pair of matte black Jeep Wranglers filled the remaining available space before the door lowered with a hum. A pretty Asian girl jumped down out of the first Jeep. She was 5'4," slender with the springy step of a gymnast.

They all greeted each other warmly but with a sincerity which came from knowing battle wasn't far away. The woman had a sing song way of speaking while her partner was literally the strong shouldered silent type. He had a broad chest and narrow waist and walked with the same bouncy spring in his step. He tossed JT the keys and walked away from us with nothing more than a nod.

"Blia, I don't know what you see in Crane," JT said with a shake of his head.

"He doesn't say nearly as much as you do but always seems to say just as much."

JT grinned good-naturedly and shrugged away the comment.

"For you, Blia, I'd take a shot at being the strong silent type."

"Yeaaah," she sang. "A wild shot."

Motown introduced me and she flicked two fingers at me with a small smile.

Just then there was a heavy knock then a random man flew face first into the garage with a yelp. With his hands secured behind his back he had no way of cushioning his fall. Crane walked in behind him with another man draped over his shoulder. He dropped him faster than a sack of spoiled potatoes.

"Caught them spying outside," he said.

"I told you, we weren't spying," the conscious man said. He turned onto his side to glare at us but the recognition that flared momentarily in his eyes belied his words.

"If I had time I might've played the whole 20 questions game with you but I don't so I'll leave you in my friend's capable hands." He stood and gestured to Crane who nodded and pulled out a wicked knife.

Motown walked to the rear of the Jeep as he said, "Let's go, Meghan I'll tell you what you need to know on the way out."

"Hold up!" the man cried.

We all turned to him. I had to remind myself that he was helping Martize pull this off so I should feel no sympathy for him.

"Listen, I was just paid to keep an eye on this spot and call when she-" he nodded his chin at me. "showed up..." That's all I know, I swear."

"So you don't know where Martize is?" Motown asked.

We could practically see his wheels spinning as he digested the question. Motown gave him all of two seconds before shrugging his shoulders and turning away.

"I'm just saying," the guy said quickly. "I don't know where he's at right now, but if you promise to let me go I'll tell you where I last saw him."

"All right, deal. You tell me what I wanna know and I give you my word I'll let you go."

"I'm just saying, last time I saw Teaser he was at this old abandoned church house up near Duluth. That's all I know, now come on man, let me go."

Motown signaled us to get in the trucks as he said, "I said I'd let you go. Crane, on the other hand, is the one who owns your ass."

He started screaming for help and thrashing around until Crane kicked him in the jaw. Crane pushed the button to open the garage doors.

It took everything I had in me not to look back.

CH15

Motown guided us to a gas station about a mile or so away from JT's. It was fully dark out and after the recent snowfall not many people were out without a reason. He jumped into my backseat.

"I've been thinking," I said, "We can go about this a few different ways since we have the element of surprise. I can call Dumb nuts and give us a head start. If Carmen's beacon hasn't moved she's probably stationary which will lend us an opportunity to sneak into wherever she is."

"Sounds like you've given this a little thought so why don't I show you some gear and we can go from there."

I hadn't thought about wearing any "gear" but I suppose it should've been obvious when Blia and Crane had shown up. Both wore unrelieved black from head to boot and the SUVs were heavily modified. Just a quick glance showed, bullet-proof armor, a highly complex digital center console, satellite/CB radio, a fold down back seat that apparently hid a storage area.

Motown opened the trap door. He pushed down on something inside and a four-sided panel popped up. On the panel pointing directly up were four different pistols with silencers and extra magazines. He rotated it and it clicked on a new face like a black ops rotisserie stick. This face was dominated by a modified AR-15 complete with suppressor, laser sight, and extra ammo. Another two swivels showed a black outfit not unlike Blia's with what was clearly built in armor of some sort and boots that were clearly my size.

"Long story short the handguns are 9mm's with a higher grain bullet that should allow you to protect yourself efficiently. Thank Blia for the specialized dark suit, she and Carmen are always going on about how women should have curvier body armor.

"I suggest wearing this beneath your clothes so you'll retain the element of surprise. I have the suspicion Dumb nuts is gonna try to make sure you're alone but I'll be in the wings somewhere."

I went into the station and changed. When I came back out Motown was studying his laptop.

"We can leave whenever you're ready." I pulled out a burner phone and made the connections to forward my number to it.

Motown grinned wanly. "I can't believe I didn't think of something so simple."

XX

20 minutes into our desperate ride to save Carmen, 50 minutes into our allotted hour, Motown's phone rang. Although we knew it was inevitable I still kind of railed at the fates. We were still about 35-40 minutes away from Carmen.

When Motown signaled I said:

"Martize you're an asshole."

"It seems we agree on this issue, however, if I find him first I'll be sure to relay your message." A familiar dark voice replied.

"Domeer?" I glanced at Motown quickly in the rearview. He shrugged, just as mystified as I was.

"Yes."

"You're an asshole, too," I blurted. "You drugged me!"

He didn't hesitate for a second, if anything his voice got darker, colder, like what the void of space might sound like.

"So that we can avoid a lengthy argument on the point, I never drugged you. The chocolate you voluntarily ate was enhanced with completely natural ingredients. Now shall we move on to why I called?"

I wanted to argue just to relieve the stress I was feeling but his stress on "voluntarily" gave me pause. Motown hadn't touched a drop of the chocolate he'd been given so maybe that should've been a warning. Ironically enough, had it not been for whatever "natural ingredients" that stimulated my system I might not have lived long enough to be angry, or embarrassed.

"Still, you could've warned me."

"Next time you drink a Mountain Dew I'll be sure to warn you there's caffeine in it. At either rate I called to warn you that your adversary and many of my competitors have begun an auction."

"I still have the package, if that's your worry.."

"Nevertheless, I'd feel better if I sent you some assistance."

"Look, Domeer, you paid me to finish this run and I intend on finishing it. There's no way your assistance" can get to me in time to be any help. You'll just have to trust me."

Motown's phone beeped with another call. "I think Martize is calling right now," he whispered.

"Domeer, I'll need to call you back, Martize is calling."

"Very well."

"Martize?"

"Hello Meghan."

"You're an asshole."

"I know and you're a bitch so now that that's settled I have a proposal. You trade yourself and your package for Carmen."

"You've been lying to me for a long time so how do I know you'll let her go if I agree."

"You don't but let's just say once I get what I want I'll have no use for her."

"Tell me where Carmen iş and I'll"

"Absolutely not. You'll meet me at the Mall in 30 minutes, alone, then we can go from there." He hung up.

"We'll have Crane drive out that way as a decoy," Motown said.

"He'll be tracking Crane's progress so we should have him stop somewhere and when Dumb nuts calls we'll say you've been pulled over. By then we'll be close enough to Carmen where it won't matter."

I hoped my plan would work without any complications even though I knew there would be no guarantees.

XX

We parked about a half mile away from an old building. From outside it looked as though it was waiting for someone to move back in. The windows, although cloudy with dust, were all intact, the roof wasn't leaning more one way or another under the weight of the day's winter's snow and there was no unwanted debris just lying around.

Motown had a night and heat vision scope on his rifle. He showed me three warm bodied sentries on the perimeter and another two bodies inside surrounding a third in a seated position.

"That's more than likely Carmen," his breath fogged in the cold air.

I nodded while trying to stop the hammering in my chest. I, we, had to save her and there was no getting around that. I had no clue what they were in there doing to her but I knew I wouldn't let her stay down there alone.

I got in the second Jeep and looked at Motown for a moment. We both took a deep breath.

He reached in, squeezed my hand, and nodded.

"Aight, let's go."

I knew this part of my plan could backfire but still I returned his nod and drove off down the road.

Armor made the Jeep slow on acceleration so I didn't get pushed back in my seat by the hand of God but I could feel the power pulse through the frame as my speed increased. I had one destination in mind; the building. I knew Motown would be taking out any guards outside that he could see while it was my job to get the truck as close to Carmen as possible and get her in it.

30 feet from the building a spot light came on, blasting into the windshield. Suddenly sharp pings started sounding off the Jeep. I swerved from instinct and cursed as my course changed but seconds later the light vanished. I knew where Carmen was and now I knew I'd be off the mark.

I only had a second to think of that as I finally crashed into the store front. Glass made way for steel then I went through a flimsy wall. A masked man thumped up onto my hood before vanishing beneath my wheels but I kept going, trying to get as close to Carmen as I could.

I stomped on the brakes as Carmen came into view. She sat slumped in a rolling chair.

Her face bruised beyond recognition and her clothes in tatters in the head lights. I pulled a pistol free and cracked the door. Dust and snow swirled around the room.

I stepped out into the room cautiously, wishing I could just run to her. She looked up at me through one slightly swollen eye and tried to speak.

"Save your strength." I choked out as I cut her hands free.

A noise grabbed my attention over the blowing wind seconds before someone stepped around an open door frame and tackled me into the Jeep. I dropped my gun as we struggled and tried to regain my balance. He reared back, smashing his head into my face as I simultaneously lashed out with a foot to his shin. With his balance off his forehead crashed into my chin instead of my nose. Ignoring the pain I whipped an elbow up into his chin then bit his nose through his mask. His holler told me exactly who he was.

Martize.

Hatred bloomed in my heart.

I grazed his groin with a swift knee but he backed away and pulled out his own pistol.

Carmen flew out of nowhere and tackled him but in her weakened state she only managed to hold him down. The gun fired twice and her body jerked with each impact. She fell away from him holding her stomach.

With no room for thought I lashed out with a boot that caught him square in the chin, knocking him to his back. I swept up his gun and pressed it clean to his forehead, pulling the trigger without hesitation.

Tears sprang to my eyes as I rushed to Carmen.

"I... love...you...Bubble gum... panties..." she gurgled while raising a shaky hand to my cheek.

"Hold on, Carmen, we have people who can help you."

But I knew it was too late when her eyes fluttered close. I hugged her as I let the tears flow. I didn't even care that someone was walking up behind me. I turned bleary eyed to find one of Martize's goons walking up on me with his submachine gun pointed my way before his head exploded in a red mist.

In that moment I wish Motown had missed.

Epilogue

Apparently the computer that Domeer planned on building would make Steve Jobs and Microsoft look like cavemen.

I finished my delivery without any further hassles and made him a very rich man in the process. I was too tired to even care. He thanked me personally but surprised me when he showed up with his wife.

It was the same matronly lady I delivered a package to not even a week ago. She had her son Hamilton with her and he gave me every bit of deference due. She glittered and gleamed as before.

"I knew you had the skills to get this done," she said with a firm hand shake. "I could tell you were special the moment I laid eyes on you."

"Thank you. Now I hope I don't have to go on any more runs this...harrowing any time soon."

She laughed. "Whether you do or don't I'm sure you can handle them."

I'm sure she was right but at the end of the day I wasn't sure I wanted to find out.

226

XX

For the first time in Naq history everybody who knew Carmen was a part of one run. It was a run where no questions were needed. A run where everyone cooperated by playing their position. But for some this was one run too many.

We stood on a bridge with her ashes in an urn overlooking the Mississippi river. It was a favorite hangout spot of hers and only those closest to her knew she wanted her ashes spread whenever this day came.

Motown stood next to me in all his solidarity. His company and presence was comforting even though I still gave him a bit of emotional distance. Alicia and E stood on my other side while many other workers surrounded us. Blia cried into Crane's stomach which gave him an almost comical look of indigestion. Everyone was here for Carmen. The love was apparent.

"Welcome to your final run," I whispered as I sprinkled her ashes.

Made in the USA
Monee, IL
25 September 2023

43414185R00134